Pop Fisher and the Shamans

Gordon T. Alston

Published by Big G Books

Cover Illustration by Nayani Gannile based on an original sketch by the author.

Printed in the United States of America

ISBN: 978-1-7332186-6-5

For everyone who enjoyed Metamorfose and encouraged me to write this prequel.

Pop Fisher
and the
Shamans

POP FISHER AND THE SHAMANS

1 CHAPTER

PETERSBURG 1965: GET IN THE HOUSE

Pop Fisher was so busy tending to his garden that he hadn't noticed the darkening clouds that were stirring up, but when he heard that horrifying chugging sound, he immediately recognized it. It had visited his house before, and so he tranced into the spirit world to confirm his fear.

He was pulled back to the natural world when his great-grandson Marcus grabbed and began shaking his hand yelling over and over, "Granddad, do you hear that? "

In a calm voice close to a whisper he said, "Yes. Boy, I need you to get in the house. Tell momma to get everybody to the basement."

1

POP FISHER AND THE SHAMANS

Not understanding the urgency of the command because of Pop's calm demeanor Marcus asked, "What is it Granddad? What is it?"

With impatience in his voice Pop pointed towards the house and said, "Marcus, I told you to get going boy."

As Marcus took off in a dash towards the house, Pop's mind drifted back to the first time he ever heard that sound.

2 CHAPTER

1890: AN EARLY INDUCTION

Akikta Catawnee knew that bringing his 7-year-old great-grandson William to the intercession ceremony would make it potentially more dangerous than usual, but he needed for him to begin to learn the things he would be expected to face when he got older. Akikta had taken his own son Wahkan, William's grandfather, to his first intercession when he was 15, and the two of them had taken William's mother Qaletaqa to her first one when she was also 15. When William began having nightmares when he was 4 years old, his mother couldn't believe they were starting at such a young age; her father and hers began when they were about 14. With William's visions starting earlier than expected, Akikta, Wahkan and Qaletaqa debated about when they should begin Williams' indoctrination into the Shaman world. They eventually agreed that it would be best to hold off acclimating him to the family's calling as long as possible.

When they did, reluctantly, finally start William's slow acclimation, they started by giving him small assignments during weather ceremonies. Then they started bringing him along on healing rituals. However, with each passing year, William's nightmare visions became more frequent and more frightening, so the three decided that his real indoctrination would have to begin now, even though he was just 7 years old, by having Akikta take the boy to his next intercession.

The intercession was for a woman whose husband had sought Akikta's help. The man had told Akikta that his wife had been having problems sleeping. He said she would wake up gasping unable to speak, and that she would be exhausted all day. He went on to say that she also began to talk to herself and hallucinate. At times, she also seemed incapable of recognizing her husband.

When Akikta arrived at the house with William, he gave William a corn husk rolled tightly around herbs and said, "follow me and do as I do."

The house was small. It had walls of woven river cane and wood covered with mud, with a roof shaped like an upside-down funnel made of grass and bark.

Akikta lit the tip of the rolled corn husk he was holding, then lit the tip of Williams husk. He began to walk slowly around the little shack of a house waving the burning husk and faintly mumbling a chant, which was hard for William to hear. Without trying to mimic his great-grandfather's chant, William followed slowly behind Akikta matching his steps as much as possible with his small legs and waving his husk in the same manner as his great-grandfather.

After they completed a full circle around the house, they then proceeded to the house's entrance, where the woman's husband met them. Looking at Akikta and then at the boy and back to Akikta again with a quizzical expression on his face, the husband said, "Thank you for agreeing to help my wife". As he led them into the house, he said, "She's in here."

She was sitting quietly at a table with the look of someone that hadn't gotten a good night's rest in days. Akikta wasn't sure what to expect when he got there but was glad to see that the woman was calm and in her right mind.

He greeted her with, "How are you doing today?"

"Exhausted, but well," she replied.

Before she could ask about the child, Akikta introduced William to them as if nothing was unusual about having a child with him, saying "This is my great-grandson, William. This is his first intercession."

The couple looked as if they were expecting Akikta to say more about the boy's presence.

Akikta wasn't here to explain his family's history, it's gifts and curses, or any of the things that necessitated William's presence, so he just looked at the couple and said, "Tell me what's been happening and when it started." As he took a seat, he pulled William next to him.

The woman looked at her husband expecting him to start, but since she seemed to be doing fairly well today, he nodded for her to go on with the story.

"About six months ago I began to feel tired and worn down. I thought it would pass, but it didn't. While there were some days where I felt better, most days I was fatigued. I tried different medicines and herbs that I was recommended to take, but nothing worked.

There were days when I would just walk around in a cloud all day, and trying to rest did nothing. Some days I couldn't even recall what I had done on those days.

Then, almost a month ago, I'm not sure if I was dreaming that I had awakened or if I was actually awake, but I saw what appeared to be and old lady standing in the shadows of our room looking at me. The moonlight gleaming through the window was enough to faintly highlight parts of her features causing the darkened parts, with their elongated shadows, to look even more frightening. Feeling exhausted and being in a semi-lucid twilight state, I couldn't scream or get a word to come out of my mouth. While I mouthed speechless words, the figure vanished through the wall."

As the woman told the story, William was as much fascinated as he was scared. He listened intently while focusing his eyes on the woman's mouth and the forms it made to produce each sound of each word, as if every contortion was somehow vital to the story. Akikta listened just as intently as the child, searching for anything that would give him a hint of what they were facing.

When the woman finished recounting her experience, Akikta said, "I think it would be best if we stayed with you tonight to try to observe, firsthand, what you are experiencing."

Hearing his great-grandfather's words, tipped William's feelings more toward fear than to fascination. Akikta didn't need to look at William's face to see the apprehension on it. He was a little apprehensive, himself, about keeping the boy with him but knew that William's increased visions are what necessitated him being there, at his young age, in the first place. In an effort to ease the boy's fear Akikta turned William towards him and said, lightheartedly, "Here is where the real fun begins." This moved William's mind back towards fascination again.

"I'll prepare a spot for you and the boy to rest," the man said to Akikta.

Leaning towards Akikta the woman reached out and touched his hand, that was resting on the table, and with a weary but appreciative look said, "Thank you for staying." Rising from the table, she said, "I'm sure you are hungry by now so I'll fix some plates."

After a supper consisting of rabbit, beans and squash, everyone settled down for the night.

It must have been the wee hours of the morning when Akikta noticed the woman sleepwalking through the house. He gently shook William to wake him and said in a hushed tone, it's time." Akikta put his finger to his lips indicating for William to be silent and motioned for him to slowly follow him as they both followed the woman. The woman's husband must have still been asleep, and not knowing how the man would react to possible events Akikta had no plans to wake him.

Akikta and William, trying to be as quiet as possible, slowly followed the woman. The woman made her way to the entrance of the house and went outside. Akikta and William were about 20 paces behind the woman when suddenly she began to take flight, arms splayed like a bird's wings, but not flapping. William's eyes widened with amazement as he quickened his pace to keep up with his great-grandfather. It was dark, but William thought he saw and old woman on the lady's back. William bumped into the back of his great-grandfather who had stopped to try to get a better look at the lady with a figure on her back, swooping and twisting and turning as she flew through the night sky. They both stood there and watched this scene for hours. Then with a dive and left turn, the lady and her rider flew right into the entrance of the house. Akikta took off into a full run heading back to the house, with William trailing far behind but doing his best to keep up.

When William came through the door, he saw Akikta slowly looking around the house, moving in the same quiet manner they had moved in earlier. With many excited words backed up in his throat waiting to come tumbling out, William knew from his great-grandfather's movements that he must remain quiet.

William was right beside his great-grandfather when they got to the couple's' sleeping quarters. As they slowly peered into the room, their eyes adjusting to the increased darkness, they could see the woman back in her bed beside her husband. Akikta gently clasped William's hand and headed back to where they had been resting. Knowing that William would have many questions, Akikta said, "We'll talk in the morning, right now we should try to get some sleep."

Having been up the whole night Akikta drifted right off to sleep, but William, having slept earlier and still filled with the excitement of what he'd just experienced, lay awake while all the questions he had for his great-grandfather swirled around in his head.

When the sun came up, William was still awake but beginning to drift into sleep. Akikta woke up and set up where he was, next to William. Akikta looked at William and assumed the boy's efforts to stay awake was him waking out of sleep. Gently shaking William into full consciousness, Akikta said, "What we saw last night was a hag riding the woman's back." He explained, "A hag is an evil female spirit, a demon. Sometimes these spirits will take over a person's body and make them do things they wouldn't ordinarily do, like harm themselves or someone else. Other times they will attach themselves to people to torment them, as we saw last night."

William couldn't remember all the wonderous questions he had had for his great-grandfather last night, so he just listened.

When Akikta heard the husband and wife stirring, he went to talk to them, and William followed. He found the couple sitting at the table waiting for them. Looking at the woman Akikta said, "Well you've had 'one' night."

With concern in his voice the husband asked, "What happened?"

Akikta responded, "We saw a spirit ride your wife last night."

Neither the wife nor the husband said a word to Akikta's response.

After he paused to let what he'd said set in, and to give the couple a chance to respond, Akikta looked at the wife and continued, "The spirit was an old hag, and it rode your back through the sky for several hours. If this is what has been occurring over the last several months, then it's no wonder you are so fatigued." He went on to explain that a hag was an evil female spirit, a demon that takes over a person's body and makes them do things they wouldn't ordinarily do, like harm themselves. He said that at other times hags will attach themselves to people to torment them.

The woman and her husband looked at Akikta in disbelief.

Eventually the woman asked, "What can you do to help me?"

Akikta said, "Since the hag only seems to be tormenting you and hasn't taken over your body, whatever we decide to do should be a lot easier than trying to remove a spirit from within you. He continued, "First we need to figure out why the hag is tormenting you. There may be something you need to do to stop it."

POP FISHER AND THE SHAMANS

William just listened as the adults talked, taking in everything that was said.

Akikta asked the woman, "Did you have a run-in with anyone several months back?"

The woman responded that she didn't remember anything happening that could cause something like this to happen to her.

Speaking to the woman's husband Akikta asked, "How about you?"

The husband's response mirrored his wife's response.

To both of them, Akikta asked, "Do you know of anything that may be going on with your family or any of your close relatives, or maybe something that happened in the past?"

The couple shook their heads no.

After asking the couple several more questions to try to uncover a reason for the haunting, Akikta told them that he would like to spend the night over the course of the next couple of days. He said that he would need to go home to retrieve some things that he would need to help with the intercession and told the couple to, as much as possible, try to get some rest today and tonight, and that he and William would return tomorrow.

When Akikta and William arrived at the couple's house the next evening, Akikta carried a satchel that he had packed with various items he thought he would need to help rid the woman of the hag.

As before, the group sat at the table to talk. Akikta asked the woman, "How did last night go?"

"I'm exhausted, so I don't think it went well," she replied.

Her husband said, "I woke to find her getting back into bed, but that was about all I saw."

Akikta inquired if either of them had managed to come up with anything they thought may have precipitated the haunting, but the couple said they still had thought of nothing. So Akikta moved on to telling them his plan for helping them.

He told them, "Sense we don't know what caused this

to happen, we'll have to see if we can find out who the hag is so that we can stop her." Reaching into the satchel he had brought with him, he pulled out a small thick green glass bottle. Handing it to the man, he said, "I want you to splash this on the back of your wife's nightgown before she goes to sleep. It's a compound made of beans, grain, and fish oil that will glow in the dark. If the hag rides your wife's back tonight, it should rub off on her and I can follow the trail she leaves."

As they had done on the first night, the group finished discussing the plan, ate supper, and settled in for the night.

In the wee hours of the morning, Akikta noticed the woman sleepwalking through the house again. He didn't bother to roust William since he wouldn't be following the woman out of the house. As before, after several hours, the woman came back in and went back to bed. In the darkness, Akikta could see tiny fluorescent droplets leading to her bedroom.

In the morning, the group met around the table and discussed the next steps Akikta was going to take. Akikta told the group, "When it gets dark enough tonight, we, referring to he and William, will see if we can see a trail of the compound outside. If we can see it, we will track it to the end and hopefully find the hag."

"What will you do if the trail does lead you to the hag?" the woman asked.

With a look of contemplation, Akikta said, "I'm not sure yet. It depends on what I find when we get there."

When night fell, Akikta, William and the couple could fully see droplets on the floor of the darkened house, droplets they hadn't been able to see before. They went outside the entrance of the house and began to look for the trail on the ground. Although the droplets were small and spaced widely apart, Akikta thought it was enough for him and the boy to track. He told the couple to proceed with their nightly routine, and that it was important that they changed nothing.

Akikta loosed his horse's reins, holding them in his hands as he and William walked slowly and looked for each set of fluorescent droplets that would hopefully lead them to the hag. Being closer to the ground, William was adept at finding the faint droplets.

POP FISHER AND THE SHAMANS

Whenever the droplets would lead in a specific direction, the two would mount and ride the horse in that direction until it looked as if the droplets had run out. Then they would dismount and walk until they found the trail of droplets again.

Akikta figured they must have gone about ten miles, when the droplets stopped at a patch of woods. Akikta tied the horse to a small tree and he and William made their way into the woods. After about fifty paces they could make out a small farmhouse in a clearing. Just as they reached the clearing, they saw a dark figure high in the sky coming toward them. The figure was flying too straight and was too big to be a bat, and Akikta thought he saw faint shimmering streaks as it flew over them and the woods they were just leaving. Seeing this, Akikta hastened his pace to the farmhouse with William, almost running, beside him. When they got to the small house, Akikta circled it, looking into the dirt-crusted windows to see inside. Finally, in a low voice he said to William, "We are going in."

Akikta found the front door unlocked, and he and William entered through it. Akikta reached into his satchel and pulled out a candle and lit it. The flames flickered shadows onto the walls as they made their way through the house. They entered a room that had a bed and dresser in it. As Akikta was taking full measure of the room, William screamed a loud scream. Akikta spun around to find William frozen in place screaming, looking at wrinkled skin hanging on the back of the bedroom door. Akikta grabbed the boy from behind and tried to cover his eyes while quieting him. Shaken himself, Akikta said calmly, "It's okay, it's okay." When everything finally calmed down, Akikta released his hold on the boy and they both stood there staring at the skin. Akikta whispered, "This must be the hag's skin." William couldn't take his eyes off it; it was so wrinkled and droopy.

Akikta reached back into his satchel and this time pulled out a piece of cloth that had been formed into a small bag with another strip of cloth tied around the top to hold the opening closed. Opening the makeshift bag, Akikta showed William a powder made of dried stick-willy and peppers. "This ought to put an end to the hag's night rides," he said. He moved over to the skin and held the head up by placing a finger in each nostril of the nose, which caused the mouth to gape open. He then began to sprinkle the powder down the opening, until the cloth was empty. He released the head and wiped his hand on his pants. He then reached into his satchel and pulled out a medium sized jar that contained a small hand-sewn doll. He opened the jar and placed it on the floor near the door that had the skin hanging from it. Then he hurried William out of the house and around to the window of the bedroom so that they could watch what would happen from a safe spot.

After a few hours, they saw the figure swoop down from over the woods and come towards the house. A few minutes later they could see the gruesome figure slipping back into its skin. A few moments after it was fully in the skin, they could see it begin to scratch itself and hear it scream in a creaky old high-pitched voice, "Skin! Skin! Don't you know me skin!" Then the spirit exited the body flying manically around the room until it spotted the little doll. The spirit went into the doll. Akikta quickly broke the window with his elbow and feverishly clambered through it to get to the jar that held the doll, and now the hag. He franticly put the lid on the jar so that the hag could not escape. With William still looking on from outside the window, Akikta decided it was best for him to go back out that way and climbed back out the window with jar in hand. He looked at William and said, "Let's go." Akikta put the jar in his satchel, and they walked towards the woods. When they got a few yards into the woods, Akikta stopped and said, "We need to bury this," as he pulled the jar back out of the satchel. He pointed to a nice-sized stick and asked William to get it, then he took the stick from William, kneeled down and began to dig as deep as he could. When he reached about three feet of depth, he wrapped the jar in the cloth that had held the powder and placed it into the hole. He refilled the hole with dirt, stamped his foot on it to compact it, and added a final layer of fresh dirt on top. He had William scatter leaves over the dirt so that the spot would blend back in with the rest of the woodland floor.

As the two rode back to the couple's house, Akikta explained to William that the powder he put in the skin was meant to make the skin irritating to the hag when she tried to put it back on. He explained that not being able to stay in the skin the hag would have to find something else to go into, which was why he brought the doll along. He said putting the doll in the jar enabled him to keep the hag trapped in the doll.

By the time they arrived at the house, the day was breaking. Akikta was eager to find out how the night went for the woman and to tell the couple that the hag would not be returning. As he knocked on the door, he put his other hand on William's shoulder and said, "You did good boy."

The woman's husband answered the door, and as they headed to the table, he explained that it had been a rough night and that his wife was still asleep. "A rough night indeed," Akikta responded, looking at William with a twinkle in his eye.

3 CHAPTER

1803: WEST AFRICAN COAST

The sun was three-fourths its way through the sky, and the group was well into working the fields when one of them, Igwebuike, saw the two men emerge from the woods that ran along two adjacent sides of the fields. As they came closer, he recognized one of them, a tall man with a beard, to be one of the traders with which their clan had traded often. The traders would bring garments and cloth made in North Africa, Flemish and French fabrics, their own woolens and linens, and Indian textiles to trade for metal, crafts, beads, and increasingly slaves. However, ever since the Ezenri (Nri priest-king) of their clan had forbidden the selling of slaves to traders, the traders visited less frequently.

Recognizing Igwebuike as one of the Elders of the tribe, the men approached him. The tall one Igwebuike recognized said in English and broken Igbo, "We need a hundred slaves."

Knowing that the trader already knew that they had stopped trading their slaves years ago Igwebuike said in Igbo and in as many English words that he had picked up over the years, "As you are aware, we no longer trade our slaves to outsiders. You have known this to be true for many years now."

The man responded, "We have been unable to get the full number of people we need and can't sail until the ship is full. I was wondering if you would make an exception. We only need about a hundred more to complete our cargo, and in return we will give you ten muskets."

"The Ezenri issued a taboo forbidding the selling of slaves to traders and his laws are immutable. Besides, the number of slaves has greatly dwindled as many of them have satisfied their debts, so there is less than fifty left," replied Igwebuike.

"I guess we'll be on our way then," the man said as he and his companion turn to leave.

Shortly after Igwebuike saw the men disappear into the thicket of trees, the two men, along with others, reappeared carrying guns. Believing the men had misunderstood him, Igwebuike approached them and said, "I'm sorry, but we have no slaves to trade for the guns."

"We don't want to trade the guns anymore," the bearded man responded, then he turned to the others and said, "Get them!"

One of the tribe members yelled, "Get to the woods!"

The men in the tribe attacked the men with the guns, using what farming tools they had, to fight them. The women and children ran towards the woods on the side of the field that was away from where the traders had entered the field.

Igwebuike lunged for the bearded man, grabbing the man's musket with both hands. The two spun around and tumbled to the dirt. Igwebuike managed to get on top of the man, fiercely pressing the man's gun against his neck. As they struggled, another trader swung the butt of his weapon at Igwebuike's head, only glancing it. A tribesman had tackled the man causing the swing to come up short.

Sporadic shots began to ring out as the traders shot at the people they could not catch.

Igwebuike felt the bearded man's Adam's apple give way as he pressed the rifle almost all the way to the dirt. As the trader despairingly gasped for air, Igwebuike rose to help the others fight. As he went to help the tribesman who had saved his head from being bashed in, he caught sight of a woman named Kambili running towards the woods dragging Abaeze, the Ezenri's son, by the hand. Then Igwebuike saw Kambili's body drop to the ground. Abaeze stood over her body staring down at it in shock.

Igwebuike took off running towards Abaeze and Kambili. Seeing one of the traders grab Abaeze,

Igwebuike ran after them. Suddenly he felt a burning fire in his shoulder, then one in his stomach. A trader, just beyond the one who had Abaeze, was crouched in the field shooting at Igwebuike. Igwebuike turned to run for the woods. Feeling another burning in his side and then one in his back, he stumbled into the underbrush of the woods. He watched helplessly as the traders gathered the members of the tribe that were still alive and walked them into the woods. Once all was clear, Igwebuike ran, as fast as his body would take him, back to his village.

With blood streaming down his bare chest and beginning to soak the loin cloth that was wrapped around his waist and between his legs, Igwebuike, frantic and injured, rushed to Chizutere's house. *An outsider looking for the Ezenri would expect his house to stand out from those of the rest of the clan, but members of the tribe knew that Chizutere's house was just like theirs, with mud walls and a thatched roof.*

When Chizutere saw Igwebuike running toward him, looking as if he were sweating blood, he readied himself for calamitous news. In the expanse of the minute or so it took Igwebuike to reach him, Chizutere's mind had run through multiple possibilities. *"Are we at war with another tribe?"* *"Are members of my clan settling their differences with violence instead of bring the matter before me?"* *"Was there an animal mauling?"*

In pain and out of breath, Igwebuike wheezed out, "They have taken many of our tribe, and Abaeze was taken too!"

Hearing the words "They have taken many of our tribe" quickened Chizutere's heart but hearing his son's name took all the breath out of him - *His son was only 5 years old*.

Mustering the composure of his position as a priest-king, Chizutere first asked Igwebuike, "How bad are you injured?"

Thinking only that he must get word to the Ezenri, Igwebuike's adrenaline masked the seriousness of his injuries. Pain now shot through his body as Chizutere's questions forced Igwebuike's mind to reassociate with his body. "I don't know. Parts of my body feel on fire," he gasped in halted heaves.

POP FISHER AND THE SHAMANS

Helping Igwebuike into the house, Chizutere called to his wife Ezinne for help. They both helped Igwebuike to the floor, then Ezine retrieved a dish of water and some rags. She began to slowly pour the water over Igwebuike's torso, washing away the blood rivulets that were streaming down his body. She gently wiped at the smudges of blood that had dried. As his wife worked, Chizutere prayed over and comforted the man. As the blood cleared, they could begin to see several small holes in his skin; one high on his left shoulder, one lower to the far right of his abdomen, one in his right side, and one on the lower right side of his back.

Chizutere went to the kitchen and began to make a salve of boiled tree bark and plant leaves. While the mixture cooked down, he returned with a jug containing mmanya ocha -a palm wine- and a knife for digging out the musket balls that were lodged in Igwebuike's torso. Chizutere and Ezine helped Igwebuike prop up his head. Holding the pitcher of mmanya ocha close to Igwebuike's lips, Chizutere said "Drink as much of this as you can," as he slowly tilted the pitcher and carefully poured the wine into his mouth. Igwebuike took small constant sips, exhaling through his nose, so as not to slow the flow of the liquid that would help dullen his senses. When the pitcher was about half empty Chizutere tilted the pitcher upright, stopping the wine's flow. As he and Ezine lowered Igwebuike's head back down, Chizutere said "We'll let you rest a minute." Ezine went to the kitchen to check on the salve and in a few minutes returned stirring and grounding the residue that was in the pot. She set the pot on the floor next to Igwebuike, whose breathing had eased because of the wine, to let it cool a bit.

To Igwebuike, Chizutere and Ezine's voices began to sound as if they were dragging every syllable of their words. Then he felt a sharp pain in the right side of his stomach. "Ohuu! Ụfụuuuuuuu!" Igwebuike's now heavy tongue dragged out as he squeezed Ezenri's hand that he was just now aware he was holding.

"I know it hurts," said Chizutere as he plucked the first of four small round metal balls from its unwelcoming hiding place. Chizutere had not given Igwebuike anything to bite on, or to muffle his cries because he knew that pain always felt better once fully released. Chizutere poured a little of the mmanya ocha into the new vacant wound, then took four fingers full of the salve and smoothed it over the wound. Next, he moved to the hole in Igwebuike's right side, digging the musket ball out, inducing more slurred yells from Igwebuike. In the same manner as before, Chizutere cleansed the wound with the wine and applied salve to it. Chizutere removed the third ball from Igwebuike's back, repeating the same pattern of dig, scream, cleanse, and patch. Chizutere saved the removal of the final sphere from Igwebuike's shoulder until the last. The other balls had been in mostly fleshy parts of Igwebuike's body, but the one in the shoulder was lodged in muscle which would be harder to remove and would hurt more. As he fished the last metal ball out of the muscle, he heard two cries of pain: one loud, now un-slurred "Ohuu!" from Igwebuike, and a loud "Aaaaah!" from Ezenri. When the salve was on the last wound Ezenri slid her hand out of Igwebuike's hand, flexing her fingers to regain circulation.

With the wine having completely worn off and the worst of the pain over, Chizutere asked Igwebuike to tell him everything that happened.

POP FISHER AND THE SHAMANS

Though weary, fueled with reemerging adrenaline, Igwebuike's words came quickly. "We were out tending the fields when two traders approached us from a thicket of trees. I recognized the tall, bearded one called Mr. Jack from our previous trades! They asked me about trading for our slaves! I told them as we had told them before, that we no longer traded our slaves to outsiders! I told them, 'You have known this to be true for many years now!' The man said that they could not leave without a full ship and asked if we would reconsider and said that they were willing to trade us guns for the additional slaves! I reminded him that you had forbidden the selling of slaves to traders over five years ago and that this taboo was immutable! To discourage further conversation, I added that since you issued the taboo, the number of slaves had dwindled, as many of them had worked off their debts. Hearing this, the men went back into the thicket of trees but returned almost immediately with other traders and guns! I told them that we had nothing to trade for the guns! That's when Mr. Jack said that they no longer wanted to trade the guns and the others began to attack us! We fought them as the women and children scattered and ran for the woods! Our farming tools were no match for their guns! They began to shoot at whoever they couldn't subdue! Kambili was running holding Abaeze's hand when they shot her! I tried to get to Abaeze as he stood over her body in shock, but before I could get there, they grabbed him! As I continued to pursue him, I felt a burning fire in my shoulder, then in my stomach! As I turned to run for the woods, I felt another fire in my side and then one in my back! I stumbled into the bush and crouched onto my hands and knees! I watched them take about seventy of the ones that they had not killed, with them! The rest of us were either dead or hiding. I scrambled to my feet and started running until I got here!"

4 CHAPTER

1803: PRECIOUS CARGO

Upon subduing each tribe member, the traders immediately put rusting iron collars around the captives' necks and shackles on their hands and feet to prevent them from escaping. The traders walked the last of their precious cargo to their waiting ship and secured each one of them in their place on stacks of pallets in the ship's hull. Each stack was seven pallets high and on each pallet were three people side-by-side on their backs. The height of the space between each pallet in the stack left only inches between the prostrate captives and the pallet above them. The stacks were arranged in three columns, port to starboard, with nine stacks extending the length of the hull from the stern to the bow. There was a two-foot aisle between each column. The center column's pallets were arranged so that the cargo's heads were pointed toward the bow of the ship and their feet towards the stern, while the columns on each side of the center column were arranged to have its occupant's heads towards the walls of the ship and their feet toward the center column of pallets. Each stack of pallets contained the members of the same tribe, in the same way that other commodities like apples are grouped together by type. This was done because over the years, slave buyers developed preferences for slaves from particular tribes. Because they couldn't trust the slave traders, the buyers from the larger plantations would often bring along a tribe member they had previously purchased to validate the pedigree of the slaves they were buying. The slave traders began stowing the captives by tribe, which allowed the traders to charge a premium price for guaranteed members of the preferred tribes.

Over the years, people from Chizutere's tribe had

become known for being more obstinate than those from other tribes, so many of the buyers from the larger plantations only purchased them if there were no others to be had. Because of the difficulty of selling members of this tribe and because there were usually plenty other, more desirable, tribes willing to trade with them, Mr. Jack and his employers took it all in stride when Chizutere had announced that he would no longer trade their slaves to traders. However, when faced with the possibility of not meeting his quota, having his commission reduced, and losing out on a bonus for filling the ship, Mr. Jack decided it was worth it to see if Chizutere would be willing to provide him with the people needed to meet the quota, even if they couldn't get a premium price for them. When Igwebuike rebuffed his plea to sell him their slaves, Mr. Jack, thinking only of the money he would lose decided to kidnap the regular tribespeople from the fields.

5 CHAPTER

1803: THE MIDDLE PASSAGE

Many of them bloodied, bruised, and terrified-
especially the children, walked in silence as their captors
led them through the jungle to the ship. While many of
them knew of the ships and the traders, they had now
become part of it. *The worst part of it!*

Ifeadigo, a tribesman around 22 years old, was the first
to speak after arriving at the ship and being huddled
into large groups for boarding. He whispered to
tribespeople around him in a soft but defiant voice, "We
will not take this voyage. When we are free of these

chains, we will escape." Some of the others nodded in agreement.

Once boarded, many were stunned when they realized the packed conditions they would have to endure. Placed on the stacks of pallets with little room to move or even breathe, still shackled, their only solace was that they were still all together.

On the first night of the voyage there was a lot of chatter, each tribe speaking amongst themselves. Some speaking of their despair and fears, others praying aloud to their gods, and some making plans to escape. After a couple of weeks at sea, in an effort to keep their precious cargo healthy, the slave traders began to take groups of captives above deck to exercise them. To reduce the likelihood of a rebellion, the traders took captives from the same level of each of the pallets, which created a mix of people from various tribes, thus hindering communication.

With the measures the slave traders put in place to prevent individual tribes from all being unchained at the same time and executing an uprising, Ifeadigo knew that there was little chance of all his tribe escaping at once. However, to keep his tribe's spirits up, he continued to plan for an escape with hopes that a situation would present itself where they could all escape. After several more weeks, during one of his night-talks, he told them, "We will have to be ready when the time presents itself." He had the strongest members of the tribe take responsibility for one child a piece, since they would not be able to escape on their own. As the days of the voyage stretched out, he encouraged his people to be patient, ensuring them that a time would present itself for them all to get away.

One day, the slave traders brought back the captives they had taken out to exercise almost immediately after they had taken them out. The traders were in a frenzied rage, pushing the group and beating them with bludgeons. When the captives were put back on their pallets, two of Ifeadigo's tribespeople were missing, as were one or two people from the other tribes' pallet stacks. That night, a woman named Ndidi, who was one of the tribespeople taken for exercise told the rest of the group that the two others leapt over the side of the ship, and that a few people from other tribes did the same after seeing them jump. After the incident, the slave traders made the captives exercise in the tight walkways between the stacks of pallets, keeping the captives below deck for the rest of the voyage. The cramped space in the hull allowed less captives to exercise at a time, which increased the amount of time they spent on their backs on the pallets. This contributed to the number and severity of illnesses that were already worsening with each day of the voyage.

By their second month on the ship, captives began to die from their sicknesses. Crew members began checking all the stacks each day before the beginning of the daily exercise schedules, for bodies of captives that had died over night. They would remove the bodies, and take them to the deck, and throw them over the ship's side.

Ifeadigo and others continued to encourage the rest of the tribe nightly with prayers and talk of an escape. "Be patient," he would say, "It is not enough for two or three of us to be free, we must all be free. We must remain patient, even in these darkest hours."

By the time the slave ship docked at Savannah, Georgia,

after the two-and-a-half-month journey, about one hundred of the captives had been lost to death.

Although Georgia officials had enacted laws in 1798 restricting Savanah's involvement in the Atlantic slave trade, many captains continued to illegally import the captives, but knew that the day would come when the illegal trade would also come to an end, and therefore they tried to make as much money as they could off these final voyages. Despite the captain's desire to keep as many captives as possible alive, he knew from past voyages that he could lose anywhere from ten to twenty percent of them. Knowing this, to be able to bring as many captives as he could to market, he always demanded that his traders secured the maximum number of people to fill the ship's capacity and he paid them commissions and bonuses for meeting the quota. He also implemented the exercising of the captives and feeding them rations of familiar foods to keep them as healthy as the cramped squalid environment would allow.

After the ships docked, the captives were taken to holding-pens not too far from the Square where they were to be auctioned. When they got to the pens, the captives continued to be aggregated by tribe. On their first night in the pen, Ifeadigo continued to encourage his tribe with his talk of escaping, the way he had done during the voyage. "We will not be in this place for long," he said." When the time is favorable, we will rise up against our captors and leave this place for home." He then set about ensuring that those adults that had survived the trip took responsibility to help the children, that had been assigned to those who had perished.

The next day, the captives became distraught as the slave traders began taking all the children from the pens. Their cries of despair could be heard back at the Square where a group of buyers had gathered for what would be a three-day auction beginning the next day. The children were herded all together, not separated by tribe, and taken somewhere else. Grief stricken himself, Ifeadigo had no immediate comforting words for his tribe as they dealt with this sudden new terror. A few hours after the children had been taken, the same slave traders came back and began to separate the remaining tribe members by perceived age. Those who looked to be in their early teens to early 30's made up one group, those that looked to be from their late 30's to early 40's formed another group, and the ones that looked to be older formed the final group. Each group was identified by strips of different colored cloth that were tied around their left ankles. In pairs, the slave traders inspected each member of a group, and made notes. Once the inspections were finished, the captives were allowed back together, but were warned not to remove the colored strips of cloth from their ankles. That night, Ifeadigo, again, talked of the plan to escape. In a determined voice, as if to will it to happen, he said, "The time is nearing when we will be able to flee this place and return home. We will find the children and we will leave!"

When the sun was high in the sky the next day, the slave traders that had carried out the inspections returned and split the tribe back into groups. They did this with each pen that held the various separate tribes. They began to pull out the things that they would use to prepare the captives for sale. For the younger groups they used animal fat to oil their skin. To give the older captives a younger look, they applied black boot polish to their skin and polished it in deeply. They also used some type of compound to whiten the teeth of those they thought needed it.

As his skin was being rubbed with black shoe polish, Ifeadigo and the other captives could hear the sounds of the crowd that was gathering in the distant square. Ifeadigo thought to himself *"This will be the day of our freedom."* Once the men who had been preparing the captives for sale left, Ifeadigo spoke to his tribe members, who were now assembled together again, without the colorful strips of material attached to their ankles. Pointing to the members that were responsible for the safety of the children Ifeadigo said, "You will look to see where each child for whom you are responsible is located and at the right time snatch them to freedom." Speaking to several members that had no responsibility for saving children Ifeadigo said, "On my signal you will began to fall over in pain as if stricken. It is during this commotion that we will fight our captors, grab our children, and flee home."

Back at the square, the children, all tribes together since the captors believed the Igbo children to be too young to have learned insolence yet, were brought to the auction block. Then the bidding began. Scared, visibly shaking, with eyes wide, a boy about the age of seven went first. Several buyers approached the boy. One looked in his mouth and stretched the boy's eyes wider open to examine them. Another poked his stomach as if the buyer was a doctor giving the child a physical exam. After the inspections ended, "Who will take this fine young buck," the auctioneer yelled. Hearing an initial bid, the auctioneer launched into very quick verbal gymnastics concluding with "Sold!" The process lasted only a few minutes but had garnered ten bids. With each new offering the process repeated itself. Some children were brought out clinging to each other and were offered as a set. Some buyers purchased several individual children. At the conclusion of the auction the auctioneer reminded the buyers that the adult auction, scheduled for the next two days, would be a Scramble. *Unlike the "Highest Bidder" auction for the children, in a "Scramble" auction, the buyers are taken to the pens where the adults are held, then when the auction begins, the auctioneer opens a pen's gate and the buyers run in and grab the slaves they want to buy and then settle the bill on the spot. While the buyers thought this form of auction was done for their sport, in actuality it was done to prevent the buyers from being able to inspect the captives too closely, increasing the likelihood that even the oldest of them, with a little polish, would be sold for a good price.*

As the time ticked on no one came to march the adults to the square and Ifeadigo began to worry a little about the execution of his plan to escape. When the sun fully set, confirming to Ifeadigo that the adult captives would not be auctioned at the square that day, his emotions were mixed. He had increased worries about the execution of his plan, but also welcomed the additional time he now had to perfect those plans, even with adjustments to them.

It was the second day of the auction. As day broke Ifeadigo and his tribespeople were anxious for the moment when they would be taken to the square. Ifeadigo couldn't stop himself from going over everyone's assignments several times before the captors arrived. Pointing to the members that were responsible for the safety of the children Ifeadigo said, "You will look to see where each child is located and at the right time snatch them to freedom." Speaking to the several members responsible for creating the distraction, Ifeadigo said, "On my signal you will begin to fall over in pain as if stricken. It is during this commotion that we will fight our captors, grab our children, and flee home." He made sure that he used the exact same words with each repetition, worried that any variance might mess up the plan.

After several hours, Ifeadigo's tribe could see a crowd gathering at one of the pens that was further down the street from where they were being held. Then, in the distance they began to see and hear a lot of commotion.

The Scramble Auction began at the pen at the head of the street that led to the Square. When the Auctioneer announced, "Open the gate," buyers rushed into the pen in a mad scramble grabbing captives. "I've got these two here," one man shouted as he grabbed two teenaged boys. "I've got this one," another shouted as he grabbed a young woman. "These four are mine," someone else shouted. It went on this way until the pen was empty.

Knowing their plan for escape, Ifeadigo and his tribe thought the commotion was from another tribe's attempt to flee. Ifeadigo worried that this might impact their plan. Angrily he muttered, more to himself than to anyone in particular, "Those fools." Ifeadigo had thought it best to make an escape once they were at the Square because the crowd would be large and there would be so many different tribes together that it would be hard for the captors to catch everyone that was escaping once the commotion began. He was counting on the other tribes to also try to flee once they figured out what was happening, which would create greater chaos. He also wanted to take advantage of the Square being closer to the Port than the pens, knowing that every additional inch mattered when it came to escaping.

When the crowd of Scramblers moved to the next pen the commotion started again and Ifeadigo was surprised that another tribe was trying to escape from their pen. *Maybe there were some successful escapes from the first pen and that is why the next tribe tried the same thing*, he thought. Buoyed by the thought of successful escapes from the other pens, he couldn't help but have a fleeting thought of changing his plan, but he pushed the thought aside knowing that his plan gave them a better chance of having the most people escape and knowing that a major part of that plan was to also save the children that had been taken from their pen the previous day.

While the second Scramble continued, a smaller group of men came to the pen holding the Igbo tribe. They lined the tribe members up and put burlap sacks over their heads, then marched them out of the pen. As the walk went on, members of the tribe wondered why it was taking them so long to get to the Square. The smell of the ocean became stronger as they continued to walk, then the ground changed under their feet and the dirt gave way to what felt like wood. They could hear the sound of the water sloshing. Then the walking stopped, and the sacks were removed from their heads. With the sacks gone, they could now see that they were not at the Square but were at the pier instead. As the men, who had taken them there, spoke with several men at the gangplank of a medium sized boat, Ifeadigo, with a heavy heart for the children they would have to leave behind, knew that this would be their best chance of escape, so he gave the signal. Several tribe members began to drop to the ground and writhe in pain, grabbing their stomachs and sides. As some of the men who had brought them there hurried to assist those who looked stricken, an argument ensued between the men left talking at the gangplank. "You are trying to sell us people that are ill!" shouted one of the men that had come from the boat. As the commotion on the pier grew, the argument at the boat turned into a fight when the men, who had been talking to the captors at the gangplank, turned to reboard their boat without the captives they were there to buy. One of the captors lunged forward and tackled one of the boat men as he headed back up the gangplank. With people running and fighting everywhere, Ifeadigo and his tribespeople began to overtake their captors, pushing a few of them off the pier and into the water. One captor began shooting wildly into the crowd of dark faces until a young tribesman got his arm around the man's neck and squeezed it until he heard it snap. A group of tribespeople pummeled another captor until his face was a mash of skin and blood. The men at the gang plank fought and shot at each other, wounding or killing a couple of people from each side. Eventually a few remaining people from the boat were able to board and pull the gangplank, leaving the last of the captors on the pier with the revolting captives.

When the last captor was either dead or in the water, Ifeadigo assembled the remainder of his tribe and said, "Let us go home." With that, the tribe ran toward the end of the pier and leapt off the end. One by one they began to soar into the sky. From a distance, to the people back at the pens, the flying Africans resembled a flock of crows high in the sky.

6 CHAPTER

1803: AFRICA

For the next several days, following the taking of his tribespeople, Chizutere spent long periods of time sitting undisturbed in a trance, searching for his people. As much as he wanted to stay in the trance until he found them, sending his spirit out of his body was taxing on both his body and spirit, so he forced himself to take breaks to recuperate after each day of searching. Also, he had never sent his spirit out for more than a couple of hours at a time, so sending it out for a day was already taking a big risk and sending it out for multiple days at a stretch could render him unable to reunite his spirit with his body.

After about four weeks, he found the heart fire of his spiritual apprentice Ifeadigo. Ifeadigo didn't know if he was awake or dreaming when Chizutere first visited him on the boat. After realizing it wasn't a dream, Ifeadigo only had time enough to give Chizutere an accounting of the adults and children that were on the ship, and to mention his desire to escape. Before his soul disappeared, Chizutere assured Ifeadigo that he would return.

Distraught by the plight of his captured people, Chizutere sought the counsel of some of the oldest members of the tribe to help devise a plan of escape for Ifeadigo and the others. He told the group of the circumstances the people faced on the ship, then solicited ideas for their escape plan. When the discussion seemed to be hitting a dead end, a woman named Sinachi said, "They could fly away as our ancestors did." Sinachi was somewhere between 100 and 110 years old, although by looking at her sturdy stature, sinewy arms and legs, and her still mostly black short-cropped hair, someone who didn't know her would guess she was in her forties. As a little girl, out of the many stories her grandmother had told her, the story that made her mind dance the most was the one of her early ancestors taking flight to escape a massacre. Through the many years of stories being passed down orally from generation to generation, some stories lost their veracity due to the number of variations that grew with each retelling of the stories to the next generation. Some of them lost their veracity due to the younger generations' inability to believe in incredible things they had not witnessed themselves. Other stories were altogether forgotten. The story of the flying ancestors suffered from both the number of variations that had grown over the years and from the later generations' inability to believe in things they had not seen with their own eyes. By the time the story reached the current generation it was mostly forgotten by all but a few of the oldest members of the tribe.

While questioning the variations of some of the stories, being the Ezenri, Chizutere never dismissed them as being wholly untrue, so he listened while Sinachi recounted the details of the story as best, she could. A couple of other elders added their recollections in places they felt were necessary. "My grandmother said that the king of a sizeable tribe had come through the region slaughtering smaller tribes and pillaging their villages. In anticipation of the coming raid, being heavily outnumbered, our people moved to a hilltop to help them counter the size of the raider tribe with a superior fighting position," Sinachi said. "From their positions in the hills our ancestors were able to hold off the intruders for weeks," she continued. She and other elders talked of various heroic skirmishes and tragic defeats. Wrapping up the story, with the twinkled-eye excitement and exhilarated breath of a child, Sinachi said "When the battle was all but lost, it is said that the last of our tribe took flight off the hill and escaped a complete massacre." Since no one had volunteered it, Chizutere, asked "But how did they do it?"

In answer to Chizutere's question, a discussion ensued where different elders theorized like scientists, taking agreed upon facts from other stories and offering them as possible answers. The theories that garnered the most support was, that they used some kind of energy from the spiritual realm, or that they were able to do it because of joint faith, or that some kind of latent gift manifested itself as a result of the crisis.

Because of Chizutere's, and preceding priest-kings', ability to trance into the spirit realm and have their souls travel great distances, he knew that any single or possibly all three of the theories could be correct. Chizutere asked the elders to remain with him to help him try to intercede for the captive tribe members. For the next couple of weeks no one left Chizutere's side as they all prayed to their ancestors. As everyone prayed, Chizutere tranced into the spirit world every day in search of anything that would confirm that his ancestors indeed flew from the hilltop, and in search of the answer for what enabled them to do it. He also continued to visit Ifeadigo, giving him encouragement with promises of escape and telling him to keep everyone else's spirit up. One day Chizutere came out of a particularly long trance. He was exhausted and his body looked drained of all its energy, but his face was that of someone that was content. After a little time to rest and eat, he informed the elders, "I was able to see a vision of that day on the hilltop. The ability to fly must have been an instinctual response for survival, long lost to our tribe. The group that flew from the hill that day, through their communal prayers and wails of suffering collectively entered the spirit realm and awakened the gift." Many of the elders thought that Chizutere's somber look and tone was from his exhaustion and/or from the ensuing task of trying to create the conditions that would enable his people to escape through flight, but there was something else that troubled him. They soon understood his somberness when he eventually said, in a voice filled with woe, "Only the adults were able to take flight from that hilltop." Thinking of all the children, as well as his own son, he vowed to himself that the children would not be left behind this time.

Chizutere and the elders spent days in communal prayer trying to tap into their ancient gift for flight. Some of the elders developed the ability to trance like Chizutere. Then, one by one they began to feel different. When the majority of the group began to feel this way, Chizutere decided it was time to try to fly. As the evening turned into night the group gathered outside. As the Ezenri and spiritually strongest, Chizutere was the first to try to fly. He ran as fast as he could and leapt into the air. He did not soar as he had expected, but he also didn't fall to the ground. His body skimmed very close to the ground, touching it at times, but otherwise gliding just above it. Excited by what they were witnessing, the others ran and leapt into the night air, experiencing mixed results. Those who initially fell to the ground got back up and tried again. Everything was a frenzy of activity as everyone repeatedly tried diving into the air. Eventually everyone was flying and testing their ability to fly higher. The evening concluded with much excitement, but Chizutere knew that the hardest part, helping the captive tribe members, who were by now far away, tap into this ability to fly, was still ahead.

Later that night, Chizutere tranced his soul to visit Ifeadigo. He explained to him the ability the tribe had once had for flight and explained what he and the elders had just achieved. They then set a plan in motion to have Ifeadigo try to get the rest of the captives to tap into their flight ability. He explained that the children most likely wouldn't be able to tap into the ability, and therefore, the adults would have to be responsible for trying to carry the children to safety. Ifeadigo informed Chizutere that the best place to escape was from the deck of the ship, but that the captives from one tribe were never all unshackled and taken to the deck at the same time. He said that although it would be difficult, he would continue to look for a way that would enable them to all escape.

Ifeadigo shared the escape plan with the rest of the captured tribe. Every night he encouraged them as they prayed and sought the spirit world and their inner ability to fly. He also prayed for a situation to present itself where they would all be unshackled at once, above deck. He warned them that even if they felt that they were able to unlock their gift, the only true time that they would be able to test it was during the actual escape.

Chizutere's soul visited Ifeadigo periodically to help him continue to work on the escape plan and find out about any progress they had made. On one of those visits, Ifeadigo told Chizutere, "Some of the members have reported feeling different inside, and feel it is a sign that they are awakening their ability to fly." Even with the tough task before them, this news still lifted Chizutere's mood a bit.

POP FISHER AND THE SHAMANS

Their plan to escape became even harder when two of Ifeadigo's tribe members became impatient and decided to try to escape during their exercise break. When they were unshackled, they ran and leapt over the side of the boat. Seeing them leap, members of other tribes also leapt over the sides. After this occurred, the captives were no longer allowed above deck.

Ifeadigo redoubled his efforts to assure his people that they would indeed get a chance to escape if they just dedicated themselves to the task of tapping into the flight instinct efforts and remained patient. In the effort to ensure their patience, he acknowledged that they may have a better chance of escape once they were off the ship.

Ifeadigo's constant encouragement, and the members' persistent prayers and progress in everyone believing they had tapped into the flight instinct, kept everyone patient until the voyage finally ended.

When Chizutere sent his soul to the ship to confer with Ifeadigo about the escape, he found the vessel empty. He didn't know how long it would take to locate

Ifeadigo's heart fire again, wherever it was, and that worried him. With each day of failing to find the heart fire, Chizutere's agony grew, and he began to wonder if he'd ever find it again. When he finally found Ifeadigo's heart fire again, it was moving fast, and it was closer than it had been on the ship. Unable to have his soul to lock onto the fast-moving heart fire, Chizutere was instinctively drawn to his village's center. When he came out of his trance and reached the center, he saw that the elders and other tribespeople were already gathering there also. It was a little girl who first looked to the sky and saw the flock of crows. As she pointed to the birds she shouted, "Look!" As everyone's eyes followed the crows, they began to realize that the black mass they were viewing wasn't a flock of crows at all, it was Ifeadigo and the captured tribespeople. The crowd broke into cheers as each person swooped down and landed. The cheers slowly quieted when people began to realize that there were no children among the returning members.

When he landed, Ifeadigo immediately sought out Chizutere. When they found each other, they clenched into a tight embrace. Ifeadigo immediately began to tell

Chizutere of the events of the escape and the unknown fate of the children.

Later that day, after celebrating the return of the captured tribespeople, the village entered a period of weeping and wailing for the lost children. As he wept for his son and the others and prayed to the ancestors for their help, Chizutere resolved himself to never give up trying to find and rescue the children.

7 CHAPTER

1803: CHILDREN FIRST

The young child didn't know what to make of his situation. Everything was so overwhelming, the attack in the fields, the long ship ride, being taken away from his adult tribe members after spending a night in a pen like cattle, then spending a second night in a pen with only children. Now, his hand clung tightly to Amaka's, a 9-year-old girl from his tribe, as the bad men walked them to the square. Shaking with fear, they walked in silence.

POP FISHER AND THE SHAMANS

Once they reached the square, the men took a few of them at a time and paraded them on a small stage. Abaeze watched, wide-eyed with frightened curiosity as throngs of men and women approached the stage, poking the children that were there, and looking in their ears, noses, and mouths. After the pokers would leave the stage, a period of yelling would ensue, followed by the children that were on the stage being led away separately by one or two of the pokers. This spectacle repeated itself over and over.

When the men took Abaeze and Amaka, and several other children that remained to the stage, Abaeze and Amaka continued to cling desperately to each other. He continued to cling to her as people poked and inspected them. After the inspection, the yelling began. When the yelling ended, an old man with rough-hewn hands but kind eyes led Abaeze and Amaka away. Although Abaeze was as frightened as ever, he was comforted knowing that Amaka was still with him.

The old man walked them to a weathered wooden wagon drawn by a mule. He muttered things to them as he loaded them into the wagon. Although they couldn't

understand him, his words seemed free of the anger
that characterized the slave traders' voices.

8 CHAPTER

EARLY 1800S: FISHER OF MEN

Jubal Fisher and his wife Annabel were part of a small
like-minded collective of three farm-families devoted to
helping captured Africans. They often pooled their
money to try to purchase the women. By purchasing the
women, they would disrupt the slaveowners' financial
strategy of expanding their slave holdings through
pregnancies, both normal and forced. The families
would alternate taking responsibility for the purchased

slaves, with one family taking the responsibility for the slaves purchased at one auction, and the others taking responsibility for those purchased at subsequent auctions. To the other slaveowners, the three-farm collective appeared to operate like all the other slaveholding farms and plantations. However, each of these families would pay the slaves a small wage for working the farm and would teach them how to read, write, and handle their finances. Once they were sure the slaves could take care of themselves, they would free them. Many of the freed slaves, owing a debt of gratitude, wanted to stay on at the farm and help continue their good work, but the three-farm collective sent them North to start new lives, and this was also done to make room for newly acquired slaves.

As usual, Jubal had arrived a day before the slave auctions were to start. It was always good to have the chance to mingle with the other buyers, because he never knew what information he might hear that would be useful to him later. The other buyers would discuss the number of slaves they held, the reasons for needing more slaves, and other topics related to their farms and plantations.

POP FISHER AND THE SHAMANS

On the first day of the auction, Jubal watched, with the internal simmering anger he always felt, as the captured children were being auctioned off. With his heart pounding inside his chest, he had mastered the same look of anticipation and glee the other buyers had on their faces, as he sought solace in the knowledge that his time to act would come on the following day. However, knowing the efforts he had made over the years, and the ones he would be making tomorrow, did not prevent the stabs of pain that shot through Jubal's nerve endings with each sale of a child.

Maybe it was the years of suppressing his emotions, or maybe it was how the two young children clung to each other, but Jubal found himself bidding on the two them.

After winning the bidding battle, he led the children to his wagon and in a comforting voice said, "You're safe now." In his heart he knew he had made the right decision to purchase the children instead of waiting for the next auction day to purchase an adult woman.

9 CHAPTER

YEARNIN' LEARNIN'

The children acclimated well to Jubal's farm. They were willing workers at each task they were assigned and acquired new skills quickly. In time, they even accepted the new names the farmer and his wife called them, "Abraham" and "Hannah Fisher." Learning to read, write and count also came quickly to them; however, as time passed, Annabel worried about little Abraham because there became periods of time where he'd just stare off into space. Initially she thought he was searching his mind for a particular lesson's answer, and she would get his attention by calling his name. Eventually, calling his name grew into having to shake his arm. However, when he started to no longer respond to her gentle shakes, she began to believe the boy was epileptic. Since these episodes were infrequent and didn't seem to harm the boy or his learning, Annabel accepted her diagnosis and continued her lessons, focusing on Hannah and leaving Abraham undisturbed until he came out of the episode.

During Abraham's first episode, everything around him went increasingly darker until it was as if he was now in another place. He could see a faint small figure far off in the distance, but couldn't make out what it was, and then the vision was over. As he got older the figure seemed to draw closer to him and his visions would last longer. By this time most of his and Hanna's formal learning was complete, and they were now learning about the workings of Fishers' efforts to save captured Africans. Although they were always told by the Fishers that they were free, it was also at this time that they were informed that they would be officially emancipated when they each reached the age of 20.

POP FISHER AND THE SHAMANS

When Abraham was 15 years old, during one of his episodes the figure finally reached him. It was a familiar face with a familiar voice, and though the face had aged and though his own memory was clouded, Abraham still recognized his father.

10 CHAPTER

SEARCHING

Chizutere sent his soul out daily in search of the captured Igbo children. With each passing year he rededicated himself to his efforts, even as the others in his tribe began to lose hope. Several years passed without success, then one evening he saw what appeared to be a faint spark far off in the distance. After finding this spark, Chizutere began spending more time out of his body in hopes of getting to the spark. Once he was even near death from having his soul outside of his body for almost 72 straight hours. It took another seven years before Chizutere finally reached Abaeze. Abaeze wasn't the 5-year-old he held in his mind's eye anymore. He looked more like a man now with well-defined cheekbones and a muscular yet lanky body frame. As they stood in front of each other, at first speechless, they could still see traces of the faces they once knew in the person that was now before them.

"I always knew I would find you," Chizutere said with subdued joy.

"I always hoped you would," replied his son.

Not wanting to waste a moment, Chizutere began pouring out his plans for Abaeze's escape. He also asked about the other children and was saddened to find out that only Amaka was with Abaeze, and that Abaeze had no clue to the fates of the rest of the children. Chizutere had to return his soul to his body, and left Abaeze happy but sad.

Chizutere returned the next day to finish planning Abaeze and Amaka's escape but was surprised when Abaeze informed him that he and Amaka wanted to stay with the Fishers to help them. Abaeze explained how the Fisher's had rescued many captured Africans and how they, themselves, were purchased by the Fishers and were being taught how to read, write, and do math, and that they weren't in bondage as were the other captured Africans. He explained how they were now working with the Fishers in their endeavors to put an end to slavery.

Chizutere reluctantly conceded to his son's wish to stay, and admired the leaders that he and Amaka were becoming. Chizutere told Abaeze he would help him from afar, as best he could, and vowed to continue his search for the other children. He also made Abaeze promise that he would also search for the other children as he helped the Fishers in their mission. Before leaving, Chizutere said that he would inform Amaka's parents of her decision to also stay and tell them of the important work that she and Abaeze were doing.

11 CHAPTER

THE EMANCIPATOR

Along with purchasing Africans at the slave markets, Jubal Fisher also purchased slaves from slaveholders who often sold some of their slaves to satisfy debts they owed or because they had otherwise fallen on hard times. No matter how hard things got, some slaveholders never sold their slaves, they instead offered them out for rent.

At first Jubal didn't involve himself with the renting of slaves, until Abraham and Hannah came to him with a way to help them also. By this time Abraham and Hannah had become a very important part of the Fisher's efforts to educate the new arrivals. They suggested Jubal rent slaves when he couldn't buy any, and then proceed to teach them ways to plan an escape so that the slaves could go back to their farms and lead others to freedom. Jubal greeted this new idea with enthusiasm and reconfirmed in his soul that there was a reason he was compelled to rescue the two of them the day he saw them clinging to each other.

The way this new endeavor would work was, when the rented slave would arrive, Jubal would pair them with Abraham or Hannah depending on their sex. Each would work alongside the rented slave and begin planting ideas of escape. The rented slave would assume Abraham or Hannah were just other slaves with thoughts of escaping and would have no idea that Jubal and Annabel were part of this effort. If the rented slaves seemed receptive, they would eventually teach them how to plan an escape. They would warn them to take their time planning the escape once they were back at their farm to ensure the best possibility of the escape being successful. The delay in time would also lessen the Fisher farm's connection to the escape.

While Abraham was working with the Fishers to free slaves, Chizutere continued to periodically visit him. Chizutere not only was checking on his son's wellbeing, but he was also intent on teaching him how to trance and use his spiritual gifts to help him in his work. When Abraham finally tranced, he sent his soul to visit one of the nearby farms that had previously rented them a slave named Ely. Ely recognized Abraham but thought it was a dream, even when Abraham explained that it wasn't. Abraham would visit Ely many times until Ely realized that it was indeed Abraham as a vision. During his out of body experiences Abraham felt a foreboding darkness all around him. The feeling was stronger at some farms compared to others. These farms were usually larger plantations or farms where the slaveholder had a reputation for being crueler than usual to his slaves.

Through his visits with Ely, Abraham coaxed and helped him prepare for escape. On the night of the escape Abraham sent his soul to be with Ely, to encourage him, and to help lead the way for as long as he could. Abraham had developed the ability to trance for a duration of about two hours without totally damaging his physical body. When Abraham's soul reached the farm that night, the darkness he had felt before had descended upon the farm, covering it in a thick dark haze. Abraham willed his soul through the haze to find Ely and the others. As he went through the haze it felt as if the darkness was rubbing bits of his soul off with a rough metal file. In his trance he concentrated on repairing the bits of soul that was being rubbed off. Never having experienced anything like this, he wondered how long he would be able to hold the trance state before becoming totally exhausted and having to return to his physical body, and he wondered if any unrepaired damage caused by the dark fog would affect him. Ely was alarmed at the site of Abraham's scarified soul. "What has happened to you?" Ely inquired. "There is a spirit that doesn't want me here," Abraham replied.

Not having stopped Abraham from reaching Ely and the other slaves, the darkness began to separate and morph into multiple demonic beings. They tried to mimic the images of the slaves, but their eyes weren't quite symmetrical on their faces. Moreover, the sclera of their eyes had a yellow hue as if the darkness could not reliably produce a white color, and being darkness themselves, their pupils were perpetually dilated. Their tongues had small almost imperceptible clefs in their tips, and their ears were misshapen as some wrestlers' ears become after years of street wrestling.

These beings mixed themselves in with the other slaves.

POP FISHER AND THE SHAMANS

In his head, Abraham could hear them whispering things to the slaves. He heard one say to the slaves it was near, "We'll get caught and lashed if we leave." He heard another whisper to a different group, "We will starve if we leave." He could hear other beings whispering things such as, "We have a good life here," and "We need to alert the overseer before we all get killed."

The fear in the group grew, and some of the slaves began to speak up about not wanting to escape and not wanting to be killed. Abraham quickly went to each group of slaves speaking words of encouragement. The words Abraham spoke were like a soothing salve to the hearts of the would-be escapees, but clanging bells in the ears of the beings with the yellow eyes. In the spirit realm, Abraham could see the beings grasp their ears in agony with each word that left his mouth. In the natural realm the beings tried to drown Abraham out yelling to their targets, "You will die if you leave! You will die if you leave!" No matter their efforts, they could not reignite the fear that Abraham had squelched. Angered even more, the yellow-eyed demons began to attack Abraham's soul in the spirit realm, but as they came at him his words became flaming bolts piercing the beings then exploding their darkness in a blast of white light. As each being exploded, their manifestations that were with the escapees disappeared. In the night's darkness, the slaves were unable to tell if the people that had just been yelling at them had walked away or just disappeared entirely; however, they were relieved and thankful that everything had returned to the calmness that had preceded the whispers.

With Abraham having calmed their fears, Ely led the escapees into the woods and on their journey to freedom. Abraham would have traveled with them, but his soul was too exhausted after his fight with the yellow-eyed beings.

12 CHAPTER

FREEDOM

When Hannah turned twenty, as promised, the Fishers officially emancipated her. The Fishers held a ceremony that resembled a graduation ceremony with Jubal and his wife Annabel speaking to all the people on the farm about Hannah's hard work and learning and encouraging the others to continue to progress toward the day of their own freedom ceremony. Not wanting to leave the work that they were doing and not wanting to leave Abraham, Hannah stayed on at the farm.

POP FISHER AND THE SHAMANS

Several years later, when it was Abraham's turn for emancipation, not only did the Fishers celebrate his emancipation, but they also performed and celebrated Abraham and Hannah's wedding. About three years after their wedding the young couple welcomed their first child, a girl they named Anna, the name was a derivative of both Annabel and Hannah. Five years after giving birth to Anna, they welcomed their second daughter Sarah, and four years after her, they gave birth to a son they named Burrell.

Abraham and Hannah taught their children as they had been taught by Jubal and Annabel. The children viewed Jubal and his wife as grandparents, and as the children grew older, they worked with the two of them and their parents to defeat slavery in any way they could.

Abraham worked to teach the children how to trance. It had taken him several years to get Hannah to the point where she could trance, and he had blamed himself for not thinking of trying to train her when they were younger. He thought training the children when they were young would be easier since young minds hadn't been taught artificial boundaries between what was possible, and what wasn't possible.

13 CHAPTER

A FAMILY BUSINESS

The Fisher farm was able to help free many captives through purchases and escapes, and Abraham's family of trancers, with the children now in their late teens and early twenties, added to their success. The dark spirits that nourished the knotted roots of slavery were strong and very deceptive. Many times, Abraham's family could see the yellow-eyed demons for what they were, as the spirits intermixed with escaping and revolting slaves sowing fear and doubt. Although every fight was difficult, being able to recognize the spirits was a plus for the family. On the night of an escape, Abraham would have the leader of the escape break the group into smaller groups, then each member of Abraham's family would be responsible for guiding, encouraging, and helping their assigned group. In every escape or revolt the family members would have to fight the dark spirits that were sure to appear.

One night, the demons had been so deceptive that Abraham and his family were unable to recognize many of them. The spirits presented themselves as willing escapees and were somehow, for the most part, able to conceal the color of their eyes. Instead of disguising itself, one particularly strong dark spirit was even able to commandeer the soul of the slave that Abraham had trained to lead the escape. The family battled the dark spirits that were unable to deceive them, however, when they thought the fight was over and headed to the surrounding woods, the spirit that had commandeered the lead escapee told the others to scatter and run. The dark spirits that had been undetected encouraged the dispersion by running and screaming for the others in their groups to follow them. The discipline and calm it takes for a likely successful escape were lost. By the time Abraham and his kin realized that this was the work of the dark spirits it was too late.

Out of the fear and confusion initiated by the dark spirits, many of the slaves made their way back to the farm. Other slaves were recaptured within the next two days by the overseer and a posse called the Trackers. The Trackers were formed by a group of local slaveowners in response to the many escape attempts being made in the area. Whenever there was an escape, the group would quickly assemble and help the slaveowner members hunt the escaped slaves. Initially the group had no name, but somewhere along the way, in the glee of hunting humans, they began calling themselves the Trackers, and would boast of the number of slaves they were able to recapture.

Abraham did not let this setback diminish their efforts to lead slaves to freedom. The family continued to battle the dark spirits as best as they could and became more successful when Burrell began to develop the ability see through the spirits' ever more complicated disguises. Although Burrell's new gift helped the family weed out many of the highly deceptive dark spirits, the escape attempts became more difficult and were still only partially successful due to the increasing number of dark spirits that were becoming able to just take over the slaves' bodies. Jubal's and Abraham's family continued to develop new strategies for improving the escape attempts. One of the new strategies that worked was infiltrating the Trackers. The farmers that were part of Jubal's Collective had men join the Trackers' posse. These men would help hunt for the escaping slaves but would find ways to sabotage the Trackers' efforts.

The escape attempts and fierce battles with the dark spirits went on for years. During this time, Abraham and Hannah's children grew up, got married, and raised children of their own. When old enough, their children also joined the fight against slavery and the dark spirits that fed it.

When Burrell's son David was born, in 1855, he had a veil of skin covering his face. Upon seeing the veil, the old mid-wife that delivered him excitedly proclaimed that a person born with a veil on their face could see things others couldn't. Still having belief in the old-wives-tails from Africa, Burrell's whole family viewed David's birth as a sign of good fortune to come. As a baby, David would babble and point at blank areas wherever he was. By the time he was three he would say enough words that his parents understood that he was seeing figures moving around. One evening, before a planned slave escape attempt that night, David asked his father, "Papa, who's that?" With no one behind him Burrell knew that David was seeing a spirit. Abraham's family could only see spirits when they were in their trance state and had never considered that the dark spirits might be near them while they were not trancing and not at the site of the planned escape. The type of fear that sets in when you realize that you survived a crisis that was unknown to you at the time of the crisis seized Burrell as he thought about all the battles they had with the dark spirits, and how they had been blind to the dark spirits' advantage of not being seen when the family members were not in the spirit realm. The thought of this misunderstood risk alarmed him so much that he suggested to Abraham and the others the need to have David with them always, so that they could see the spirits outside of the spirit realm. Having

POP FISHER AND THE SHAMANS

David see and describe the spirits he saw while following his family around the farm swung the advantage back to the family, with the dark spirits not realizing they were now being seen on the human plane.

All the work of the Fishers and the farm collective, and others like them around the country, was making a great impact over the years. A good number of the escaped slaves joined the abolition movement and bolstered its efforts by telling of the horrors of being enslaved and having pictures made of their scars. A few of the former slaves became great orators and would attract huge crowds wherever they spoke of their stories and the inhumanity of slavery. The printed stories, oration engagements, and pictures garnered increasing support for the move to abolish slavery. It was in these last throws of slavery that the dark spirits fought their hardest to uphold the demonic institution they had spawn and grown years ago.

Although the number of successful escapes began to increase, things all around them were getting worse. When David turned eight-years-old many of the states that practiced slavery, including theirs, succeeded from the United States Government and formed their own government called the Confederacy, then war between the two sides ensued. During this time, the strength and number of dark spirits increased, increasing the danger of leading escapes. After much discussion about the increased danger, it was decided that the risk to the whole family and all the escaping slaves had grown so great that there was a need to start bringing David along on the escape attempts so that he could help them identify any possible unknown threats. David's grandmother Hannah insisted on the responsibility of making sure David was safe, while the other family members continued to be responsible for the safety of small groups of escaping slaves.

Abraham and his family didn't know it but the final battle they would have with the dark spirits came on the night they first brought 8-year-old David along with them. All during the day David described the different dark spirits that were following the family and the others preparing for the night's escape. The number of spirits following them this day was far more than David had identified on any of the previous days he had helped his family, so everyone expected and planned for a tough battle. They hoped the dark spirits being unaware that they were being seen by David in the human realm was the advantage that would help this escape fully succeed.

When night came, the family members tranced into the spirit world and joined the slaves that were planning to escape. There were almost double the number of spirits than there were at the last escape. All the ones that had been following around the people at Fisher farm were there. Although the dark spirits were trying more complicated ways to conceal themselves, with David there the family was able to identify exactly who they were, even the powerful spirit that had attached itself to the leader of the planned escape. This dark spirit seemed even more powerful than before and radiated a darkness that enveloped everything within a few feet of it. With the advantage of knowing exactly which escaping slaves were dark spirits and which were not, Abraham's strategy was to split them up and fight them in smaller groups. To get the spirits separated, Abraham had sets of his family members lead their groups across the fields taking different routes. Being the strongest of the family members, Burrell took the group that included the leader of the escape so that he could be the one to take on the strongest darkest spirit. Burrell's mother Hannah was with his group also, since it was safer for David to be with her and Burrell, and safer for Burrell to have someone with David's powerful gifts there -even if he was only a child- when Burrell's battle with the strongest dark spirit began.

As the groups struck out for the fields, with David having identified them all before the groups split up, the family members began to surreptitiously eliminate the dark spirits that were traveling with them, one by one, before they had a chance to start sewing fear in the escaping slaves. Once the dark spirits caught on to the clandestine battle being waged by the family members, all-out fighting broke out. With the dark spirits' numbers already diminished, the family members had an overall easier time defeating them. However, Burrell's group not only had the strongest dark spirit in it, but several of the other ones were also stronger than the group had expected.

When the fighting broke out in his group, Burrell lunged

straight for the strong spirit. The spirit opened its mouth, stretching its grotesque blistered lips wider than its head. It was as if its whole head had split open. Out of its dark cavernous throat, over its black leathery tongue with its forked tip, spewed millions of flying cockroaches in a thick stream, right at Burrell. Using his words, as the family had done before, he shot lightning back at the spirit, blowing holes through the swarm of cockroaches. Although his lightning was annihilating the roach stream, the stream was preventing any of the bolts from reaching the dark spirit. Hannah, who was in fierce battles of her own, fighting the lesser dark spirits as they tried to frighten the escaping slaves into scattering, saw Burrell's fight and wished she could help her son, but she already had more on her hands than she could handle.

 Burrell let out a loud grunt-like roar and one massive bolt of lightning shot from his mouth, obliterating the cockroach stream, and knocking the dark spirit off its feet. Burrell jumped on it, straddling its heaving chest. Like a wrangler trying to break a wild horse, Burrell managed to get one hand hooked into the creature's opened lower mouth and held on as its body bucked, jerked, and jumped. Burrell's hand burned as he held on to the spirit's skin. Before Burrell could summon another mega-lightning bolt, the creature's leathery tongue grew and wrapped around Burrell's body like a boa constrictor, pinning his arms to his side, squeezing, and burning him. Then Burrell heard a loud piercing sound. A sound that he imagined was the sound of the Archangel Gabriel blowing his horn. Then there was a flash of blinding white light and Burrell felt the creature's grip turn to ash, freeing his arms. When he was finally able to regain his normal sight, Burrell saw his son David standing several feet in front of him, with a white energy glow outlining his body. The boy's fists were clinched, and he was heaving heavily. Looking beyond David, Burrell saw the escaping slaves and his family members standing throughout the field, in piles of ash, bewildered.

About two months after the escape, word reached the Fisher farm that the President had proclaimed that all persons held as slaves within the rebellious states were free.

Both now in their mid-90s, Jubal and Annabel Fisher had

not thought that they would be around to see the day that all their efforts paid off. When they got the word of the slaves being freed, they celebrated as if they were back in the prime of their lives.

After the end of slavery, Abraham's family found themselves being requested by the slaves they had helped to escape to help them with other situations that required supernatural help. While many in the family pulled back from the spiritual battles to focus on other endeavors, Burrell's family, being the strongest, focused their efforts on continuing to help the former slaves through spiritual intercessions.

14 CHAPTER

THE 1880S: IT TAKES ONE TO KNOW ONE

By the time David reached adulthood, he and his father had conducted numerous spiritual interventions, many of them related to remnants of the slavery demons. They also dealt with curses, hexes, and all other sorts of evil conjuring. During these years they also discovered that there were people amongst the original natives of this country, called Shamans, that would not only conduct spiritual intercessions for people needing them, but that they could also intercede with nature to coax rain from the clouds and crops from fallow land. The natives were connected to nature the way David had been told his ancestors in his homeland were connected to nature. When David turned twenty-five, wanting to reclaim the connection to nature and possibly increase the strength of his already strong gifts, he decided it was time to leave his family to seek out the most revered Shaman in the area, named Akikta Catawnee. David explained to his family that by getting Akikta to help him further develop his spiritual gifts, David would be able to be more effective at battling the dark spirits his family had battled for years, and he might also be able help the rest of the family develop their gifts too. Supporting David's desire, the family prayed for him and sent him off with their full blessings.

Akikta, his son Wahkan, and Wahkan's daughter Qaletaqa were considered the strongest spiritual leaders in the Eastern Band of the Cherokee Nation. Their family had remained in the area, along with other members of the Cherokee Nation, after the Indian Removal Act forced their people from their lands. When Akikta met David, he could sense his spiritual power. Much like his own power, he felt David's power emanating from his line of ancestors, and from their connection to their homeland. The Catawnee family was as excited to learn from David as David was excited to learn from them. Akikta invited David to lodge with him, and over the next several weeks they learned of each other's family histories. They moved on to recounting the many spiritual battles they had fought, then began to delve into explaining their individual spiritual gifts and the source of those gifts. They were delighted to discover that many of their gifts were similar, springing from a place rooted in their ancestry. Their trancing into the spirit world was exactly the same. While David's description of his tribe's ability to fly amazed the Catawnees, having ancestors who had reincarnated as other animals, and having experienced many other supernatural acts, tempered their astonishment.

After a few months of learning from each other, Akikta invited David to join him and his family for an intercession. A farmer had reached out for Akikta's help because the farmer's once fertile land was yielding less and less good crops with every new season. Akikta knew that this type of intercession would help David develop his connection to the land and nature.

POP FISHER AND THE SHAMANS

When the group arrived at the Farmers land, they walked to the field nearest to them. The meager crop it had produced had been harvested and all that remained were small nubs of stalk. Akikta removed corn husks, that were rolled tightly around herbs, from a sack he was carrying, and handed one to each member of the group. He instructed David to just follow what the others were doing. Akikta lit the tips of the rolled corn husks, and the family began to spread out over the field, walking slowly, waving the burning husk in the air, and chanting a prayer in their native tongue. Qaletaqa took David with her and followed each line of the prayer with a translation for David's benefit. The prayer translated to,

"O Great Spirit, lean to hear my feeble voice.
You have given us soil that should produce a great harvest.
Here I stand, and the soil has become infertile.
Nourish it that it may once again give life to the seeds that are planted.

O Great Earth, O Grandfather, you were here before us.

May the sun bring you renewed energy by day,

POP FISHER AND THE SHAMANS

May the moon softly restore you by night,

May the rain quench your thirst,

May the breeze blow new strength into you,

May your health be restored."

This ritual was repeated in each field on the farmers property. By the time they reached the third field, David was able to remember most of the prayer, and by the time they were at the fourth field, he began to feel nature communicating to him in his spirit. The ground under his feet that had been hard and uneven now seemed to cushion his every step. The air around him began to sing a song that was soothing to his soul. He could feel energy surging into the land.

When they were finished, David felt exhilarated, and couldn't stop talking about the feeling he had experienced. The Catawnees knew this feeling, and they were very happy that David had gotten to experience it too. They also knew that the next intercession would probably not be as pleasant as this one but, based on David's descriptions of the spiritual battles he had fought, they knew he would not only be okay but that he would be a valuable asset.

15 CHAPTER

A DYNAMIC DUO

David indeed was a valuable asset in battle. His ability
to see dark spirits in and outside of the spirit world
made the intercessions dealing with demons easier than
the Catawnees were used to; however, the battles were
still tough. David and Qaletaqa found a fighting partner
in each other. Their skills were complimentary to each
other's skills, and their instinct for what each other
needed in the midst of fighting was exceptional.
Because of the closeness they had developed through
fighting together, it was of no surprise to anyone when

that close relationship grew into love. Qaletaqa's father Akikta presided over her and David's wedding. A few months following the wedding, Akikta presided over David's induction into Shamanism. About a year after their marriage, David and Qaletaqa welcomed their son William into the world. The consecration ceremony for the baby brought together the Catawnee and Fisher families for the first time ever. The ceremony incorporated aspects of, both, Cherokee and African rituals. When the group tranced into the spirit realm together while praying, they saw William's life playout into the future. There were places where the visions split into multiple possible streams, but all the streams ended at the same point.

16 CHAPTER

A FAMILIAR FOE

When Akikta arrived at David's house, David thought that behind Akikta's usual stoical expression were troubled eyes. Akikta greeted David and Qaletaqa and lifted the now three-year old William into his arms. As Akikta play-wrestled with the boy in his arms, he began to explain the reason for his visit.

"I just came from meeting with people from a town about a three-hour ride away from here," he began. "They said that they have been experiencing an increase in hostilities toward them from persons unknown to

103

them." He continued, "While in their town, I could feel that this was more than the night riders we've heard about, that have begun to periodically terrorize some isolated farms. I could feel a heavy spirit presence that unsettled my soul like never before." Lowering the squirming child to the floor, Akikta said, "I know this will be a tough one, but I told the people that we would help them." Having already faced many extreme situations ever since he was a child, David shrugged a little and asked, "When do we go?" Akikta responded, "I told them I would return by week's end." He added, "I spoke with Wahkan before I came here, so it will be the four of us." Grabbing William one more time and hoisting him into his arms, Akikta kissed him on his cheek, then put him back down and said goodbye to everyone.

The group spent the next three days preparing for the work ahead. Early Friday morning, the group of four left David with a neighbor and headed for the town. On the ride there, David couldn't help but rejoice in the beauty of the surrounding scenery of trees, tall grasses, flowers, and streams, but disquiet at the pit of his soul reminded him that this was not a pleasure outing.

POP FISHER AND THE SHAMANS

When they arrived at the town, there was a contingent of town leaders gathered in front of a store waiting for them. A man named Elijah, one of the men that had originally met with Akikta, told them that they could stable their horses a little further down the street. After taking the group of Shamans to the stables, Elijah walked them back to the store and took them to a room in the back of the store where the other town leaders had assembled. The leaders took turns describing for the Shamans all the incidents that had been occurring. A man named Jason gave an account of witnessing someone destroying one of his fields. "I was returning from visiting a relative late one night when I saw what looked like small fires in one of my distant fields, so I rode toward the field to see what was happening," he explained. "By the moonlight I could see numerous shadowy figures moving in the field with torches. I steered my horse near a tree and dismounted. I took my rifle, and crept a little closer to the field, then crouched down and began firing at the figures. I'm not sure if it was the flickering flames from the torches or the light of the moon, but as the figures dispersed, many of them appeared to just disappear, leaving only about four of them to ride off on horses." Another man, named Tom, chimed in with, "The same thing happened to me! I heard my sheep and headed to their pen to check on them. When I got near the pen, I could see outlines of people amongst the sheep. I yelled and shot off a few rounds into the air, then leveled my rifle in the direction of the pen and squinted to try to get a better view of someone to shoot. My sheep went running out of the gate someone had opened, but there was no sign of the figures I saw in the pen." The others in the room told similar stories.

After hearing all the stories, Akikta told the men that their ceremony would take several days to complete because it would include going to each farm, business, and house in the town to pray. Elijah said that the group would be staying at his place and left with them to get their horses.

The next day, Akikta, Wahkan, Qaletaqa and David made their way from one place to the next, praying, and waving cornhusk-wrapped incense. They repeated this ritual over the course of a few days, leaving at the break of dawn and returning to Elijah's house after sundown.

POP FISHER AND THE SHAMANS

Going into and out of the spirit realm for such long periods each day was wearing on the quartet, and by the fourth day they were physically and spiritually exhausted. They were glad it would only take one more day to finish their work. After eating supper and settling in for the night, they were awakened by a ruckus outside Elijah's house. Everyone in the house hurriedly made their way to the front porch, some in thrown-on day-clothes, and some still in their nightclothes. They saw a mob of about 20 people with torches, yelling obscenities, and approaching the house from about 40 yards away. Akikta told Elijah to take his family out the back door and to not look back. As the crowd got closer, David could see that it was made up of mostly dark spirits, and he alerted the others to this fact. Akikta pulled out a sack that contained a salt mixture and poured it in a line in front of the house. This would prevent the dark spirits from getting to the house. Akikta then retrieved poles and cornhusks, that he had brought along, from the house and handed them to the others. The poles were made from tree limbs about 4 inches in diameter and 7 feet in length. The cornhusks were wrapped around a special mixture of certain roots and plants that Wahkan had prepared, and they were soaked in kerosene. Although David didn't need these instruments, he took them anyway and attached the husk to the pole as the others were doing. Qaletaqa lit the tips of everyone's husks on fire, and the four spread themselves along the salt line and slowly approached the oncoming spirits, with their homemade flaming spears leading the way.

As they came face-to-face with the mob, Qaletaqa was the first to engage with one of the mob members. She jabbed her spear forward and one of the beings in front of her let out a pained cry. Her spear must have found one of the human participants. Each Shaman fought five or six beings at a time, swinging and jousting their flaming spears, and using them to block the swings of their foes' torches. To make quick work of their battle, David began using his words to shoot lighting from his mouth to obliterate the demons. Suddenly, a large dark mass appeared and began spewing millions of flying cockroaches at the Shamans. David hadn't seen anything like this since his first fight as an 8-year-old. Ever since that first fight, David had believed that there were no other dark spirits with the strength and powers of the one he had helped his family defeat, because there was never one in the many battles that had followed. David aimed his lightening words at the spirit to stop the stream of swarming cockroaches. As the cockroaches cleared, David saw the dark spirit clearly. He remembered its grotesque blistered lips. He remembered its black leathery tongue with the forked tip. He remembered the scene of his father straddling the demon's chest like a wrangler trying to break a wild horse, as its body bucked, jerked, and jumped. He vividly remembered the fear he felt when the spirit wrapped its tongue around his father's body and began burning him while squeezing the life out of him. He remembered letting out a piercing scream and then seeing only ash. This could not be the same dark spirit, he reasoned to himself, but it was. David tried to summon and channel the power that emanated from him the night he thought his father would be killed by that demon, but couldn't, so he did as is father tried to do. Shooting a continuous stream of lightening, he ran toward the demon and jumped on it. Avoiding the tongue that almost killed his father, David hooked his hand into the creature's opened lower mouth, while the creature bucked and jumped. Summoning a mega-lightning bolt, David shot the bolt straight down the demon's throat. Having dispensed with the other dark spirits, Akikta, Wahkan, and Qaletaqa ran to help David. As David shot mega-bolt after mega-bolt down the creature's throat, it jerked violently trying to shake David loose and trying to get its tongue around him. Just as the other Shamans reached the demon and lunged their spears at it, everything turned to black smoke. When the smoke cleared, the demon and David were gone.

17 CHAPTER

THE 1890S

On the ride home, feeling proud of himself for helping his grandfather dispense with the hag, William asked Akikta to tell him about his father again. Although he was only three years old the last time he saw his father, William still had vivid memories of him doing father and husband type things around the house. He remembered all the times they played and could still hear in his head the sound of his father's voice emphasizing a lesson that should be learned from something his father was trying to teach him. William remembered the loving way his father and mother interacted with each other. The stories William wanted Akikta to tell him, were the ones he had not experienced, the ones where David assisted Akikta, his mother, and grandfathetr during exciting intercessions like the one he had just helped his grandfather conduct. Ever since David's last battle, Akikta made it a point to teach William about David and the powers he wielded during battles. Akikta always ended each story by telling William that he too would develop great powers and become a powerful Shaman just like his dad. The one story that Akikta had not told William yet was the one recounting the battle during David's final intercession. He and his daughter would tell William that story when he was much older. The only thing they told William pertaining to that day was the loss of his father, and the only thing William remembered was the sorrow that permeated the family's life, for what seemed an eternity to William's three-year-old mind.

As they rode, and Akikta recounted David's heroics during the many family intercessions, William pictured himself beside his father wielding the same powers his father was wielding. William's heart was full of pride that he was able to help Akikta the way David had once helped the family during intercessions.

18 CHAPTER

PETERSBURG, VA 1965

Even in the basement Pop's family could hear the awful chugging sound of the tornado.

"I'm scared mamma," His great-grandson Marcus said to his mother Gail, in a trembling voice. His mother quieted him, knowing he knew better than to talk while they were waiting out a severe storm, and while his great-grandfather was in the midst of prayer. They had been through this drill numerous times.

William "Pop" Fisher was rocking back and forth

mumbling something of a prayer. Hearing the boy's voice broke Pop's concentration, and without opening his eyes he said, "Boy you better be quiet while the Lord does his work." With a diminishing voice, he added, "The Lord works in mysterious ways," then he went back to his incantations. Pop prayed unceasingly, until the storm was over. When the tornado had passed, the basement where they were huddled was still intact, and everyone felt a sense of relief. Although you couldn't tell it by his exhausted, yet calm demeanor, Pop felt the most relief.

As everyone left the basement to survey what damage was done upstairs and to the rest of the neighborhood, Pop Fisher thought of all the other times he had dealt with situations like this. Watching Marcus ascend the stairs, he thought back to the time when, as a child himself, he assisted his grandfather with an intercession and how they captured a hag. He thought about the nightmares that continue to this day. He thought about his family helping him discover his abilities and helping him to hone them as he grew older. He thought about how he progressed to assisting the whole family with intercessions, as they trained him to be a Shaman. He thought about his mother, grandfather, and great-grandfather finally telling him the full story about his father when they thought he was old enough to handle the grief. He thought about the many battles he and his family had fought together. He thought about the battles he fought and continued to fight alone, and he thought about the ones he thought he could avoid by having decided not to take on the mantel of Shaman.

19 CHAPTER

1903: A FULL ACCOUNTING

The family had just finished a particularly long and tiring intercession dealing with a spirit that had possessed a woman's husband. As they sat around discussing the day's events, Akikta decided it was time to give William a full recounting of the day his father was taken from him. After all, William was now 20 years old and had developed a full understanding of the risks that he and his family faced when helping others. William also had developed a better understanding of his own powers and abilities. As they finished the accounting of the day's events, Akikta said, "William it's time we give you all the details of the day we lost your father."

Akikta described to William the scene of David riding the demon like a cowboy trying to break a bucking bronc, and him shooting a lightning bolt straight down the demon's throat. Akikta explained how just as he, Wahkan, and Qaletaqa came to help David, everything turned to black smoke, and how when the smoke cleared, there was no sign of his father or the demon.

Although William had always had general knowledge of his father's death during a fight with demons, having his grandfather describe the scene in such vivid detail filled him with pride, but also left something unsettled in his spirit.

20 CHAPTER

THE DECISION

After a couple of minor intercessions through the end of the year, Akikta decided it was time to make William a full-fledged Shaman. He discussed his decision with William's mother and grandfather, and they agreed that this would be a good time to conduct the ceremony. However, when they informed William of the decision, his lack of enthusiasm caught them off guard. Then William told them of his desire to one day raise a family free of the burdens of being a Shaman. The family accepted William's decision but advised him that having

POP FISHER AND THE SHAMANS

a spiritual gift was a burden in and of itself and told him that the dreams he had been having since he was a child would probably continue until he fulfilled his destiny. William hoped, to himself, that that destiny was to live a normal life.

21 CHAPTER

1910: YOU CAN RUN BUT YOU CAN'T HIDE

It had been a little over six years sense he had made the decision not to follow the rest of his family into Shaman-hood, and William was happy with the simple life that he and his new wife Violet were living; establishing a farm and working to expand it. However, one evening a lady came to William's farm asking him to help her gravely ill 4-year-old son Franklin. Seeing the boy's condition, he yelled for Violet to go get a doctor. Hearing this, the woman interrupted him saying that the boy had already seen a doctor and that the doctor was unable to help him. She explained that she believed the illness was due to a generational curse put on the family that would manifest with the first born of their son's generation, and that their son was the first born of the generation, and that what she needed was a Shaman to intercede for her son. William told the woman that he had relatives that could help her, but the woman said that she had already gone to them and was told that they were away and wouldn't return for several days, and that she was told that he was the only other person that could help her son. William had the woman lay her son on a bed so that he could examine the boy. William could see that the boy's legs were immensely swollen. He asked the woman how long they had been swollen, to tell him of about any other symptoms, and to tell him about the generational curse she thought he was under. The lady said, "The swelling started about two weeks ago and got progressively worse. Besides pain, he has been very lethargic, and has been unable to leave his bed for about over a week." She then began to tell William the story of the generational curse that was put on the family as the result of something his great-great-grandfather had done, and then she gave a quick history of the family. William moved the boy to a blanket on the floor, then retrieved and lit a cornhusk incense, and began praying over the boy while running his hands over the boy's legs. He then pulled out two silver dimes, and using a sticky substance, placed one dime on the bottom of each of the boy's feet. After about an hour, the dimes turned jet black. William explained to the woman that the black dimes confirmed her suspicion that her son's illness was caused by a curse or hex. William opened a jar that had what looked like salt in it. He proceeded to pour the salt on the boy's legs, and within minutes, splits appeared in the boy's legs and began to ooze blood that was almost black. Then out of the slits ran small black snakes. William chased the snakes around the room, using the lit end of the incense to burn them, turning them into ash. He then had Violet bring a basin of water into which he poured a small vial of liquid and proceeded to wash and bandage the leg wounds.

After the healing of Franklin, William found himself periodically being petitioned by others for help when no one else was available to help them. At first William resisted the help-seekers' pleas, telling them to wait until one of the real Shamans in his family was available; however, this did not dissuade people from continuing to seek his help. Increasingly, the people being brought to William for prayer, healing, and intercession were children, and having a heart for children William reluctantly resigned himself to helping them. Although he had turned away from officially becoming a Shaman, helping the children satisfied something within him. As the number of children that he had helped increased, people began to refer to the group of children as "William's kids," and eventually, began affectionately calling William 'Pop Fisher'. William officially became a father when Violet gave birth to a baby girl they named Willie, after William, because they had wanted a boy.

It had been many years since his healing of Franklin had pulled him back into using his gifts to help others, when he answered a knock at his door and found himself face to face with the now grown Franklin, Franklin's wife, and their daughter Gail. After greeting each other, Franklin told Pop Fisher that he needed his help. Franklin began to explain that the generational curse that had almost killed him as a child had been manifesting itself in different ways as he was growing up. He described, to Pop Fisher, unexplained mishaps, extended periods of misfortune, and terrible recurring nightmares. He said that until recently the nightmares were only about him, but now included his daughter. He said that he feared for his daughter's well-being and wanted Pop Fisher to intercede on her behalf. Having already saved Franklin's life and having an understanding of the curse, Pop agreed to intercede on the girl's behalf. Pop Fisher had the family move to a bedroom and put the girl on the bed. He lit a cornhusk incense and walked around the room waving it, filling the room with a light haze of smoke. When he was done waving the incense, he began to pray. As Pop crossed into the spirit world while in a trance-like state, he began to see the child's future unfold. Her future split into many different paths, and down each path he could see various versions of the generational curse manifesting itself in Gail's and her progeny's lives. While in the trance, Pop not only had seen the child's future, but saw his own family's future, and other children's futures that were somehow intertwined with Franklin's family's future. He felt the presence of a strong spirit attached to each path, and it became clear to him that this one intercession was not enough to change the outcomes of the paths. Resolving himself to the role he saw him and his family playing in the visions of the future, Pop Fisher told the parents that the only way to keep the child safe was for them to leave her there. The couple was distraught, but knowing that disobedience was what caused the family curse, they heeded Pop's words. Pop didn't tell the couple all the visions he had seen or about the intertwining of his and their lives, but he did tell them that there would be other children facing similar circumstances whose lives were connected to Franklin's family's future, and that, somehow, their parents will find their way to the couple. Pop said, "When these families do find their way to you, you will need to send them to me. Pop cautioned to only send them during a certain hour of the night, and devised a special knock for them to use so that he knew who had sent them.

Pop Fisher and his family took Gail to raise as their own child, and Pop set out to protect her and alter the futures he saw.

POP FISHER AND THE SHAMANS

A few years after the Fishers took in Gail, the special knock that Pop Fisher had devised came on the door late one night. It was a woman who told Pop that she was told that he could protect her daughter. Pop accepted the girl without question. He didn't need, or even want, the backstory, all he needed was the special knock indicating the person doing the knocking was sent to him by someone he trusted.

Other children would follow, always starting with a late-night syncopated knock at the door. The Fisher family integrated these "door-nock" babies into their family. Although she was only in her late teens, Pop's daughter Willie took on the primary role for raising Gail, and later, Gail took on responsibility for raising some of the new "door-knock" children. With other family members taking responsibility for different children, all the children grew up as brothers, sisters, cousins, aunts, and uncles, all believing they were blood relatives, and in some cases, they were actually blood-related although not as they thought.

22 CHAPTER

PETERSBURG VA: I'M BUILDING ME A HOME

The Fisher household was getting crowded and Pop Fisher's ability to protect everyone was getting tougher with each new addition. Pop found himself in the spirit world interceding for the children more than he found himself in the natural world running his farm, so he decided it was time to sell the farm and it's now too-small house. Not only would he build a home that could hold everyone, but every material he would use for it would fortify the house with metaphysical properties to give it spiritual strength so that the house itself would provide protection for the family.

As Pop Fisher set about building his house, he used Maple wood to build the structure of the house. The Maple was used to provide strength and endurance to the house and the people within it. He used it also because the wood was thought to exude generosity, balance, and promise.

He used Cedar wood for the walls and roof, because he knew that Cedar was regarded as the "Tree of Life," or "Holy Tree," for many Native American tribes and held special spiritual significance. The Native-Americans used it extensively in ritual ceremonies and burned it to cleanse areas. A Cherokee legend explained that the Creator placed the spirits of their people in Red Cedars, and they believed the wood carried powerful protective spirits.

For the woodworking within the house, Pop used boards of Birch, Walnut, Cherry, and African Blackwood. He used Birch because of its powers of purification, and its symbolization of protection, fertility, and new beginnings. He used Walnut because of its symbolization of clarity and focus, gathering of energy, and of beginning new projects. He used it also because it was supposed to assist in letting go of unwanted associations and in making a transition or shift in a person's life. He used Cherrywood for its purification properties, and its ability to banish negative energy and reverse or halt spells or hexes. He used the small amounts of African Blackwood he reclaimed from a flute that he was told was from his father's ancestor's land, because the wood was said to act as a medium between the physical and spiritual realms. Its energy did not live in the realm of the living, and as such, it was associated with communication with the afterlife.

It was important to Pop Fisher to have a basement to the house as a place of refuge if all else failed. After the house was completed, Pop would usher the family into the basement at any sign of a storm, no matter the storm's severity or lack thereof. The family would sit silently in the darkened candle-lit basement while Pop Fisher prayed, then would reemerge once Pop said it was okay to go back up to the main floor.

POP FISHER AND THE SHAMANS

Although this new home was not a farm, Pop did build a chicken coop, and planted a large garden. The garden was about fifty yards from the house and had a fence around it made of shiny chicken wire and wooden posts that were seven feet high. It had a big gate that Pop put a lock on to keep the younger children out of it. Almost every inch of the garden had something growing on it. There were tomato plants, watermelon vines, cucumber vines, string beans, cabbage, and a section for herbs and other plants that Pop Fisher used for spiritual and medicinal purposes.

23 CHAPTER

PETERSBURG VA 1965: WEATHERING THE STORM

By 1965 the Fisher household included Pop Fisher, his daughters Willie and Lauri, Willie's daughter Gail with her husband and seven kids, and Lauri's husband and their twelve kids. The younger kids always called Pop Fisher grandad although he was their great-grandfather, because everyone else in the house mostly called him Pop. Outside of the children that were born in the house, most of the family younger than Willie did not know their true familial relationships, and those relationships were further obscured by the natural close relationships forged from everyone living in the same house with one authority figure.

The Fisher house was still strong but was so weatherworn from the many storms that it endured, that anyone who saw it assumed it had been built over a hundred years ago. The storm that came this day came out of nowhere. It was a sunny, mildly warm day with clear skies, and Pop Fisher was out in his garden with his great-grand-son Marcus, pulling weeds and inspecting the plants. As Marcus chattered on, as kids do, Pop hadn't the noticed darkening clouds, but suddenly felt a bad presence. Then he heard the horrifying chugging sound he had heard on two other occasions and knew what was to come. Turning his attention away from what Marcus was saying, Pop began to move into the spirit world. Pop Fisher saw the spirit that had attacked his extended family many times, since Pop had become their protector. In the past, the spirit appeared in different forms each time it attacked, but always with the properties of a tornado. Once it appeared as a giant bear intent on devouring the clan, and another time it appeared as an eagle ready to pick apart their flesh. This time the spirit appeared with a demonic looking face, but Pop Fisher knew the essence of the spirit and knew the spirits were one in the same. Pop Fisher's adrenaline raced as he relived his previous battles with the spirit and thought of how narrowly he had prevailed. Pop was pulled out of the spirit world when Marcus almost yanked his arm off while shouting, "granddad, do you hear that!"

Mustering up a calm voice, to hide his fear from the boy, Pop responded, "Yes. Boy, I need you to get in the house. Tell momma to get everybody to the basement."

"What is it Granddad? What is it," Marcus shouted.

Pointing towards the house, Pop said in a stern voice, "Marcus, I told you to get going boy.".

Marcus took off in a full run, almost falling as he turned the corner around the little backyard where they kept chickens. Marcus' mother Gail and everyone else had heard that awful freight train sound and were already going into the basement, after turning off all the lights and the stove, as they had done many times over. Out of breath, Marcus followed them, and Pop Fisher joined them a few minutes later.

Even in the basement everyone could hear the chugging sound of the tornado. While everyone sat silently crowded in the southwest corner of the basement, faces lit only by the flickering flames of the candles, Pop Fisher sat a little ways away from the rest of the family, rocking back and forth mumbling an unintelligible prayer. The only clear words he spoke were the ones he used to quiet Marcus, before resuming his incantations. While Pop Fisher's body was in the basement, his spirit was out in the storm.

In spirit form, Pop Fisher flew directly toward the swirling storm. As he got closer, the demonic face with menacing eyes, and opened laughing mouth showing sharply pointed teeth, and a pointed chin with a beard, appeared in the twisting clouds. Then an appendage reached out and swatted at Pop Fisher. In the same manner that he had been able to avoid the bears claws and eagle's talons, Pop swoop low, close to the ground, then fired a ball of light at the demon's head. A second tentacle swung at Pop but missed. Pop continued to dodge the blows of the demon while attacking it on all sides. Fighting this form of the demon was harder than fighting its last incarnations, and Pop Fisher was becoming exhausted from the duration of the fight, from the amount of time he was out of his body, and probably from his now advanced age. With whatever energy he had left, or just sheer will, Pop Fisher mustered the strength to soar high above the demonic storm. With his spirit beginning to glow bright white, he opened his mouth and shot a beam of light into the eye of the storm, causing the winds to dissipate and the demonic face to disappear.

In the house, the family could hear the windows rattle and the frame of the house creak as it tried to stand its ground against the violent wind whips. As they remained huddled in one corner of the basement, Gail quietly hummed "We Shall Not Be Moved." Then after what seemed like an eternity, everything fell silent. There was no creaking, no rattling, and best of all, no chugging sound of the tornado. Gail stopped humming and everyone set in silence for a few minutes more, until Pop Fisher spoke, saying "It's over."

As the family filed out of the basement, everyone

looked around in amazement at how little damage there was. There were broken windows and some picture frames off the wall. The dining room tablecloth was jumbled at one end of the table, being saved from hitting the floor only by the chair that sat at the head of the table. There were also various papers strewn about, but all-in-all, things weren't in as bad a shape as they had imagined. However, as they walked out onto the front porch, they could see piles of rubble up and down the road where houses used to stand. Some of the neighboring houses were missing their top floors, others were missing everything down to the ground. Fences were ripped up and wrapped around whatever had stopped them from blowing completely away. Some cars were moved from where they had been last parked, while others were flipped upside-down or onto their sides. The view was the same from the back porch. The tornado had done a great deal of damage to almost every house but had skipped the Fisher house.

24 CHAPTER

AFTER THE STORM

It had been a couple of months since the tornado had struck, and the process of cleaning up and rebuilding the neighborhood was well underway and had lifted the mood in the neighborhood; however, Pop's spirit was troubled. Pop decided it was time for a family meeting, and he gathered the family together in the living room. When everyone was settled, Pop Fisher, with a look of resoluteness, said, "It's been decided that Gail and her family are going to go to DC". The adults accepted Pop's edict the way they had accepted all his edicts over the years, with closed mouths and adherence. The children seemed confused but dared not to ask any questions. Some of the children cried.

25 CHAPTER

PROTECTION FROM AFAR

It had been about eight years since Gail and some of her children left the Fisher home and moved to Washington DC. Pop Fisher interceded on their behalf every day since the move, and things at both households had been fairly calm until he sensed a massive storm. The storm wasn't heading for his house in Petersburg but was heading for Gail's home in DC.

Pop Fisher sent his spirit to investigate the storm and saw the spirit whose attacks he had thwarted in the past. As in the past, the spirit appeared as a tornado, but this time, instead of appearing with the face of a bear, eagle, or demonic person, it had the face of all three. Seeing the three together, Pop Fisher realized that the spirit hadn't been morphing between personas but were three separate parts of one spirit that was now combined. Fighting the separate personas was hard enough, and now at 90 years of age he would have to do battle with the full spirit.

Although the storm appeared to be headed towards Gail's house, just to be safe, Pop Fisher returned his spirit to his body, then called for his family to go to the basement. When his second daughter Lauri complained that there weren't any signs of a storm, Pop admonished her that when there is a storm on the horizon it can be deadly from far away, even if everything looks calm. The family members did as Pop ordered and executed the drills, they had executed many times over, but this time Pop Fisher did not go to the basement with them, instead he when to the front porch, sat in a rocking chair and began his intercession.

Pop Fisher's spirit went after the storm that was approaching DC. As before, Pop Fisher attacked the storm, circling around it and making sure to avoid hits from the storm's whips. As Pop readied himself to soar above the storm, and hit it with a beam of light, the storm dissipated on its own.

Pop Fisher was relieved that he was able to get the storm to disperse without expending all his energy, but something didn't sit right with him. Considering the power the spirit had exhibited in each of its personifications, although it was difficult, the fight wasn't the challenge that Pop had expected. To be safe, Pop Fisher stayed in the spirit world watching over both houses. He watched his family in Petersburg as they huddled in the basement of the house, he had built to help protect them. He watched Gail's son Marcus, in DC, as he and a friend met outside after the rain and ventured to the site of a partially demolished factory. He watched the pair as they explored the site and saw them when they came upon the freshly made pond the rain had created in the basement of the partially demolished building. Pop could see large metal containers, like the kind that hold heating oil, floating on top of the construction pond. As he watched Marcus' friend Joseph jump from one container to the next with

POP FISHER AND THE SHAMANS

Marcus following him, he spotted something deep in the murky water. As he swooped down to get a closer look, he saw what appeared to be a glowing arm flip the container on which Marcus had just jumped. As the hand reached to pull Marcus under the water, Pop Fisher's spirit entered the water and shot a bolt from his hands that severed the arm. He moved to rescue Marcus, but the arm regenerated and wrapped itself around his waist. As he struggled to free himself, Pop Fisher managed to shoot a beam of light that surrounded Marcus keeping him afloat and giving him the ability to continue to breathe. While Marcus was suspended in the light bubble, Pop wrestled with whatever had a hold on him. Shooting rays from his mouth and eyes now, Pop Fisher was able to free himself from the monster's grip and start to obliterate the monster with each hole he blasted in it. After defeating the monster, Pop Fisher swam toward Marcus, but a whirlpool appeared blocking his path, and the whirlpool had the faces of the bear, eagle, and demon. Pop Fisher knew that this would be the fight he was expecting earlier in the day. Pop Fisher immediately began to shoot the menacing spirit whirlpool with his rays, but the rays were having little effect on it. Pop started swimming counter to the whirlpool's rotation, hoping to reduce some of its power, but being supernatural, the whirlpool's spin wasn't slowed at all. Pop swam faster and faster until he was a blur in the water, shooting a steady beam of light at the spirit's faces while he swam. Using this tactic, Pop Fisher was able to split the faces horizontally in half; however, each place that was severed rejoined itself to its other half not long after Pop's beam had severed it.

Already weakened from the first battle and weighing his ability to win this second more intense fight, Pop Fisher stopped swimming and directly confronted the spirit in the whirlpool, yelling, "Why are you seeking vengeance upon this child?" Pop Fisher already knew the reason he was protecting Marcus was due to a family curse, but he wanted to know why the spirit was holding Marcus accountable for his family's deeds while he was still only a young boy. As the whirlpool whirled without attacking, Pop Fisher continued, "I have seen the boy's future paths and in some of them he chooses, on his own accord, to repay his family's debt. I beg you to give him the time to mature into adulthood and fulfill his destiny." The whirlpool stopped spinning and Pop Fisher could see the three faces of the spirit clearly, even in the murky water, then the faces faded. Exhausted, Pop Fisher swam to Marcus' bubble and pushed Marcus towards the water's surface and lifted him high enough out of the water for Joseph to be able to grab Marcus' outstretched hand. When he was sure Marcus was safe, Pop Fisher's spirit faded from the water. As Pop Fishers' spirit slowly floated towards his body back in Petersburg, Pop could see Marcus's future, a future with only one path. Then he could see all the paths that he and his descendants had traveled to get to this point in time and knew that he had fulfilled his destiny.

Back in Petersburg, after spending hours in the basement with no sign of a storm and no further instructions from Pop Fisher, Willie Fisher led the family out of the basement. As the family went out the front door to find Pop Fisher and to see if there were any signs of a storm, they found Pop Fisher sitting in his rocking chair, eyes closed, with a peaceful look on his face. The official diagnosis for Pop Fisher was that he had died of natural causes at the age of 90.

ABOUT THE AUTHOR

Gordon T. Alston was born in Petersburg, VA, the fifth of seven children. When he was one year old his parents David and Gilbertha Alston moved the family to Washington, DC where he was raised. After attending DC Public Schools, including H.D. Woodson Sr. High, he received a bachelor's degree from The University of the District of Columbia and a master's degree from Howard University. He is the author of three children's books (*1-2-3-4 Aidan Likes to Explore*, *Anika's Pickle Pie, and The Day the Geese Came.*), and a novel (*Metamorfose*). He currently resides in Columbia, MD with his wife Nicole and their two children Anika and Aidan.

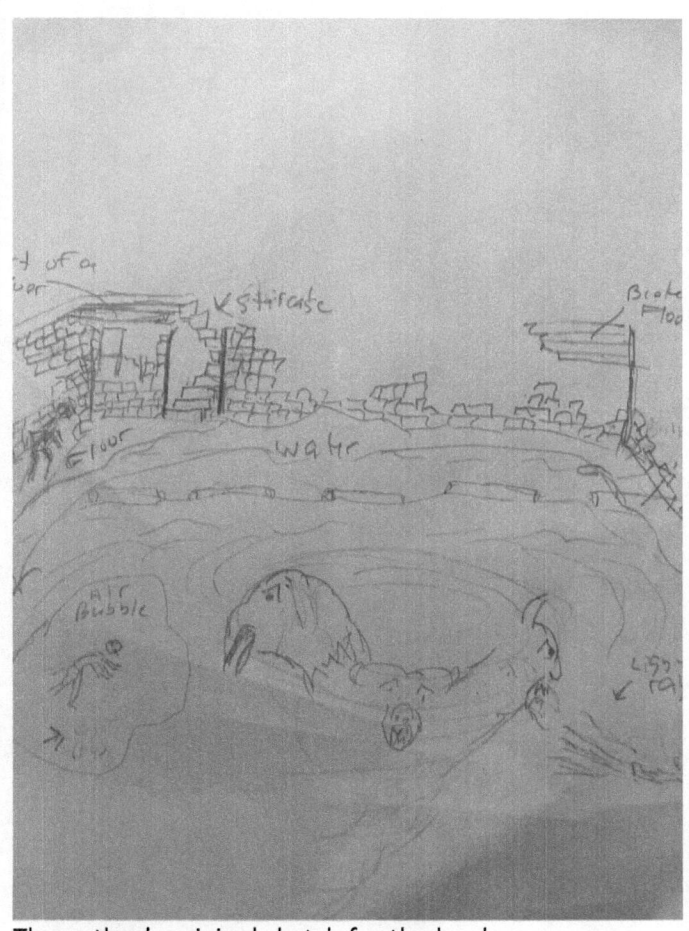

The author's original sketch for the book cover.

OTHER BOOKS BY THE AUTHOR

POP FISHER AND THE SHAMANS